"Everything is ruined."

Jessica shivered as she spoke. "My dress, my shoes, my hair . . ."

"You're only wet from the rain," Carter said gently as he led her into the bathroom. "I think your hair looks gorgeous—all wild and exotic. You should wear it down more often. It's an incredible turn-on." He took off his jacket and began rolling up his sleeves.

"What are you doing?" Jessica asked, her eyes drawn to his finely corded forearms.

"Getting you dry," he said, reaching for a towel and hunkering down before her.

Jessica shivered again, this time as much from a building anticipation as from the effects of the rain. "I'm a mess," she muttered, a little embarrassed by her sodden appearance . . . and by his nearness.

Carter grinned. It was a dangerously attractive grin that swept away Jessica's discomfort. "Any more of a mess and I'd lay you right down on the floor and make love to you here. . . ."

Jessica returned his smile, a hint of mischief in her eyes. "Maybe," she whispered, "everything isn't ruined, after all. . . ."

Dear Reader,

Welcome to Crosslyn Rise, a majestic estate on the North Shore of Massachusetts and the setting for Barbara Delinsky's long-awaited trilogy; three love stories that stand alone, but together create a powerful saga of six lives linked by a common dream. The Crosslyn Rise trilogy appears in three consecutive months, beginning in October with *The Dream* and followed in November and December with *The Dream Unfolds* and *The Dream Comes True*.

Harlequin Temptation is proud to feature these dynamic, passionate romances from one of our finest authors, and we'd love to hear your comments. Please take the time to write to us.

The Editors
Harlequin Temptation
225 Duncan Mill Road
Don Mills, Ontario, Canada
M3B 3K9

CROSSLYN RISE

The Dream
BARBARA DELINSKY

Harlequin Books

TORONTO • NEW YORK • LONDON
AMSTERDAM • PARIS • SYDNEY • HAMBURG
STOCKHOLM • ATHENS • TOKYO • MILAN

Published October 1990

ISBN 0-373-25417-2

1

JESSICA CROSSLYN lowered herself to the upholstered chair opposite the desk, smoothed the gracefully flowing challis skirt over her legs and straightened her round-rimmed spectacles. Slowly and reluctantly she met Gordon Hale's expectant gaze.

"I can't do it," she said softly. There was defeat in that softness and on her delicate features. "I've tried, Gordon. I've tried to juggle and balance. I've closed off everything but the few rooms I need. I keep the thermostat low to the point of freezing in winter. I've done only the most crucial of repairs, I've gone with the lowest bidders, and even then I've budgeted payments—" She caught in her breath. Her shoulders sagged slightly under the weight of disappointment. "But I can't do it. I just can't do it."

Gordon was quiet for a minute. He'd known Jessica from birth, had known her parents far longer than that. For better than forty years, he had been banker to the Crosslyns, which meant that he wasn't as emotionally removed as he should have been. He was deeply aware of the fight Jessica had been waging, and his heart went out to her.

"I warned Jed, you know," he said crossly. "I told him that he hadn't made adequate arrangements, but he just brushed my warnings aside. He was never the same after your mother died, never as clearheaded."

Jessica couldn't help but smile. It was an affectionate smile, a sad one as she remembered her father. "He was *never* clearheaded. Be honest, Gordon. My father wrote some brilliant scientific treatises in his day, but he was an eccentric old geezer. He never knew much about the workings of the everyday world. Mom was the one who took care of all that, and I tried to take over when she died, but things were pretty far gone by then."

"A fine woman, your mother."

"But no financial whiz, either, and so enamored with Dad that she was frightened of him. Even if she saw the financial problems, I doubt she'd have said a word to him about it. She wouldn't have wanted to upset him. She wouldn't have wanted to sully the creative mind with mention of something as mundane as money."

Gordon arched a bushy gray brow. "So now you're the one left to suffer the sullying."

"No," Jessica cautioned. She knew what he was thinking. "My mind isn't creative like Dad's was."

"I don't believe that for a minute. You have a Ph.D. in linguistics. You're fluent in Russian and German. You teach at Harvard. And you're published. You're as much of a scholar as Jed was any day."

"If I'm a scholar, it's simply because I love learning. But what I do isn't anything like what Dad did. My mind isn't like his. I can't look off into space and conjure up incredibly complex scientific theories. I can't dream up ideas. What I do is studied. It's orderly and pragmatic. I'm a foreign language teacher. I also read literature in the languages I teach, and since I've had access to certain Russian works that no one else has had, I was a cinch to write about them. So I'm published."

"You should be proud of that."

"I am, but if my book sells a thousand copies, I'll be lucky, which means that it won't save Crosslyn Rise. Nor will my salary." She gave a rueful chuckle. "Dad and I were alike in that, I'm afraid."

"But Crosslyn Rise was his responsibility," Gordon argued. "It's been in the family for five generations. Jed spent his entire life there. He owed it to all those who came before, as much as to you, to keep it up. If he'd done that, you wouldn't be in the bind you are now. But he let it deteriorate. I told him things would be bleak if he didn't keep on top of the repairs, but he wouldn't listen."

Jessica sighed. "That's water over the dam. The thing is that on top of everything else, I'm having plumbing and electrical problems. Up to now, I've settled for patches here and there, but that won't work any longer. I've been told—and I've had second and third opinions on it—that I need new systems for both. And given the size and nature of Crosslyn Rise . . ."

She didn't have to finish. Gordon knew the size and nature of Crosslyn Rise all too well. When one talked about installing new plumbing and electrical systems in a home that consisted of seventeen rooms and eight bathrooms spread over nearly eighty-five hundred square feet, the prospect was daunting. The prospect was even more daunting when one considered that a myriad of unexpected woes usually popped up when renovating a house that old.

Shifting several papers that lay neatly on his desk, Gordon said in a tentative voice, "I could loan you a little."

"A little more, you mean." She gave a tiny shake of her head and chided, "I'm having trouble meeting the payments I already have. You know that."

"Yes, but I'd do it, Jessica. I knew your family, and I know you. I'm the president of this bank, humble though it may be. If I can't pull a few strings, give a little extra for special people, who can I do it for?"

She was touched, and the smile she sent him told him so. But his generosity didn't change the facts. Again she shook her head, this time slowly and with resignation. "Thanks, Gordon. I do appreciate the offer, but if I was to accept it, I'd only be getting myself in deeper. Let's face it. I love my career, but it won't ever bring me big money. I could hurry out another book or two, maybe take on another course next semester, but I'd still come up way short of what I need."

"What you need," Gordon remarked, "is to marry a wealthy old codger who'd like nothing more than to live in a place like Crosslyn Rise."

Jessica didn't flinch, but her cheeks went paler than they'd been moments before. "I did that once."

"Chandler wasn't wealthy or old."

"But he wanted the Rise," she said with a look that went from wry to pained in the matter of a blink. "I wouldn't go through that again even if Crosslyn Rise were made of solid gold."

"If it were made of solid gold, you wouldn't have to go through anything," Gordon quipped, but he regretted mentioning Tom Chandler. Jessica's memories of the brief marriage weren't happy ones. Sitting forward, he folded his hands on his desk. "So what are your options?"

"There aren't many." And she'd been agonizing about those few for months.

"Is there someone who can help you—a relative who may have even a distant stake in the Rise?"

"Stake? No. The Rise was Dad's. He outlived a brother who stood to inherit if Dad had died first, but they were never on the best of terms. Dad wasn't a great communicator, if you know what I mean."

Gordon knew what she meant and nodded.

"And, anyway, now Dad's dead. Since I'm an only child, the Rise is mine, which means that no one else in the family has what you'd call a 'stake' in it."

"How about a fascination? Are there any aunts, uncles or cousins who've been intrigued by it over the years to the point where they'd pitch in to keep it alive?"

"No aunts or uncles, but there's a cousin. She's Dad's brother's oldest daughter, and if I called her she'd be out on the next plane from Chicago to give me advice."

Gordon studied her face. It told her thoughts with a surprising lack of guile, given that her early years had been spent, thanks to her mother, among the North Shore's well-to-do, who were anything but guileless. "I take it you know what that advice would be?"

"Oh, yes. Felicia would raze the house, divide the twenty-three acres into lots and sell each to the highest bidder. She told me that when she came for Dad's funeral, which was amusing in and of itself because she hadn't seen him since she was eighteen. Needless to say, she was here for the Rise."

"But the Rise is yours."

"And Felicia knew we were having trouble with the up-keep and that the trouble would only increase with Dad gone. She knew I'd never agree to raze the house, so her next plan was to pay me for the land around it. She figured that would give me enough money to renovate and support the house. In turn, she'd quadruple her investment by selling off small parcels of the land."

"That she would," Gordon agreed. "Crosslyn Rise stands on prime oceanfront land. Fifteen miles north of Boston, in a wealthy, well-run town with a good school system, fine municipal services, excellent public transportation... She'd quadruple her investment or better."

His eyes narrowed. "Unless you were to charge her a hefty sum for the land."

"I wouldn't sell her the land for *any* sum," Jessica vowed. Rising from her seat, she moved toward the window. "I don't want to sell the land at all, but if I have to, the last person I'd sell to would be her. She's a witch."

Gordon cleared his throat. "Not quite the scholarly assessment I'd expected."

With a sheepish half smile, Jessica turned. "No. But it's hard to be scholarly when people evoke the kind of visceral response Felicia does." She slipped her hands into the pockets of her skirt, feeling more anchored that way. "Felicia and I are a year apart in age, so she used to visit when we were kids. She aspired to greatness. Being at the Rise made her feel she was on her way. She always joked that if I didn't want the Rise, she'd take it, but it was the kind of joking that wasn't really joking, if you know what I mean." When Gordon nodded, she went on. "By the time she graduated from high school, she realized that her greatness wasn't going to come from the Rise. So she went looking in other directions. I'm thirty-three now, so she's thirty-four. She's been married three times, each time to someone rich enough to settle a large lump sum on her to get out of the marriage."

"So she's a wealthy woman. But has she achieved that greatness?"

Wearing a slightly smug what-do-you-think look, Jessica gave a slow head shake. "She's got lots of money with nowhere to go."

"I'm surprised she didn't offer to buy Crosslyn Rise from you outright."

"Oh, she did. When Dad was barely in his grave." Her shoulders went straighter, giving a regal lift to her five-foot-six-inch frame. "I refused just as bluntly as she offered. There's no way I'd let her have the Rise. She'd have it sold or subdivided within a year." She paused, took a breath, turned back to the window and said in a quiet voice, "I can't let that happen."

They were back to her options. Gordon knew as well as she did that some change in the Rise's status was necessary. "What are your thoughts, Jessica?" he asked as gently as he could.

She was very still for a time, gnawing on her lower lip as she looked out over the harbor. Its charm, part of which was visible from Crosslyn Rise, not two miles away, made the thought of leaving the Rise all the harder. But it had to be faced.

"I could sell off some of the outer acreage," she began in a dubious tone, "but that would be a stopgap measure. It would be two lots this year, two lots next year and so on. Once I sold the lots, I wouldn't have any say about what was built on them. The zoning is residential, but you know as well as I do that there are dozens of styles of homes, one tackier than the next."

"Is that snobbishness I detect?" Gordon teased.

She looked him in the eye without a dash of remorse. "Uh-huh. The Rise is Georgian colonial and gorgeous. It would be a travesty if she were surrounded by less stately homes."

"There are many stately homes that aren't Georgian colonial."

"But the Rise is. And anything around it should blend in," she argued, then darted a helpless glance toward the ceiling. "This is the last thing I want to be discussing. It's the last thing I want to be *considering*."

"You love the Rise."

She pondered the thought. "It's not the mortar and brick that I love, not the kitchen or the parlor or the library. It's the whole thing. The old-world charm. The smell of polished wood and history. It's the beauty of it—the trees and ponds, birds and chipmunks—and the peace, the serenity." But there was more. "It's the idea of Crosslyn Rise. The idea that it's been in my family for so long. The idea that it's a little world unto itself." She faltered for an instant. "Yes, I love the Rise. But I have to do something. If I don't, you'll be forced to foreclose before long."

Gordon didn't deny it. He could give her more time than another person might have. He could indeed grant her another, smaller loan in the hope that, with a twist of fortune, she'd be able to recover from her present dire straits. In the end, business was business.

"What would you like to do?" he asked.

She started to turn back to the window but realized it wouldn't make things easier. It was time to face facts. So she folded her arms around her middle and said, "If I had my druthers, I'd sell the whole thing, house and acreage as a package, to a large, lovely, devoted family, but the chances of finding one that can afford it are next to nil. I've been talking with Nina Stone for the past eight months. If I was to sell, she'd be my broker. Without formally listing the house, she'd have an eye out for buyers like that, but there hasn't been a one. The real estate market is slow."

"That's true as far as private buyers go. Real estate developers would snap up property like Crosslyn Rise in a minute."

"And in the next minute they'd subdivide, sell off the smallest possible lots for the biggest possible money and do everything my cousin Felicia would do with just as little care for the integrity of the Rise." Jessica stood firm, levelly eyeing Gordon through her small, round lenses. "I can't do that, Gordon. It's bad enough that I have to break apart the Rise after all these years, but I can't just toss it in the air and let it fall where it may. I want a say as to what happens to it. I want whatever is done to be done with dignity. I want the charm of the place preserved."

She finished without quite finishing. Not even her glasses could hide the slight, anticipatory widening of her eyes.

Gordon prodded. "You have something in mind?"

"Yes. But I don't know if it's feasible."

"Tell me what it is, and I'll let you know."

She pressed her lips together, wishing she didn't have to say a word, knowing that she did. The Rise was in trouble. She was up against a wall, and this seemed the least evil of the options.

"What if we were to turn Crosslyn Rise into an exclusive condominium complex?" she asked, then hurried on before Gordon could answer. "What if there were small clusters of homes, built in styles compatible with the mansion and tucked into the woods at well-chosen spots throughout the property?" She spoke even more quickly, going with the momentum of her words. "What if the mansion itself was redone and converted into a combination health center, clubhouse, restaurant? What if we developed the harbor area into something small but classy, with boutiques and a marina?" Running out of "what ifs," she stopped abruptly.

Unfolding his hands, Gordon sat back in his chair. "You'd be willing to do all that?"

"Willing, but not able. What I'm talking about would be a phenomenally expensive project—"

He stilled her with a wave of his hand. "You'd be *willing* to have the Rise turned into a condominium complex?"

"If it was done the right way," she said. She felt suddenly on the defensive and vaguely disloyal to Crosslyn Rise. "Given any choice, I'd leave the Rise as it is, but it's deteriorating more every year. I'm long past the point of being able to put a finger in the dike. So I have to do something. This idea beats the alternatives. If it was done with forethought and care and style, we could alter the nature of Crosslyn Rise without changing its character."

"We?"

"Yes." She came away from the window to make her plea. "I need help, Gordon. I don't have any money. There would have to be loans, but once the cluster homes were built and sold, the money could be repaid, so it's not like my asking you for a loan just to fix up the Rise. Can I get a loan of the size I'd need?"

"No."

She blinked. "No? Then you don't like the idea?"

"Of the condo complex? Yes, I do. It has definite merit."

"But you won't back me."

"I can't just hand over that kind of money."

She slid into her chair and sat forward on its edge. "Why not? You were offering me money just a little while ago. Yes, this would be more, but it would be an investment that would guarantee enough profit to pay back the loan and then some."

Gordon regarded her kindly. He had endless respect for her where her work at Harvard was concerned. But she wasn't a businesswoman by any stretch of the imagination. "No financial institution will loan you that kind of money, Jessica. If you were an accredited real estate developer, or a builder or an architect, you might have a chance. But from a banker's point of view, loaning a linguistics professor large amounts of money to build a condominium complex would be akin to loaning a librarian money to buy the Red Sox. You're not a developer. You may know what you want for the Rise, but you wouldn't know how to carry it out. Real estate development isn't your field. You don't have the kind of credibility necessary to secure the loan."

"But I need the money," she cried. The sharp rise in her voice was out of character, reflecting her frustration, which was growing by the minute.

"Then we'll have to find people who *do* have the necessary credibility for a project like this."

Her frustration eased. All she needed was a ray of hope. "Oh. Okay. How do we go about doing that and how does it work?"

Gordon relaxed in his chair. He enjoyed planning projects and was relieved that Jessica was open to suggestion. "We put together a consortium, a group of people, each of whom is willing to invest in the future of Crosslyn Rise. Each member has an interest in the project based on his financial contribution to it, and the amount he takes out at the end is commensurate with his input."

Jessica wasn't sure she liked the idea of a consortium, simply because it sounded so real. "A group of people? But they're strangers. They won't know the Rise. How can we be sure that they won't put their money and heads together and come up with something totally offensive?"

"We handpick them. We choose only people who would be as committed to maintaining the dignity and charm of Crosslyn Rise as you are."

"No one is as committed to that as I am."

"Perhaps not. Still, I've seen some beautiful projects, similar to what you have in mind, done in the past few years. Investors can be naturalists, too."

Jessica was only vaguely mollified, a fact to which the twisting of her stomach attested. "How many people?"

"As many as it would take to collect the necessary money. Three, six, twelve."

"Twelve people? Twelve strangers?"

"Strangers only at first. You'd get to know them, since you'd be part of the consortium. We'd have the estate appraised as to its fair market value, and that would determine your stake in the project. If you wanted, I could advance you more to broaden your stake. You'd have to decide how much profit you want."

Her eyes flashed. "I'm not in this for the profit."

"You certainly are," Gordon insisted in the tone of one who was older and wiser. "If the Rise is made into the kind of complex you mention, this is your inheritance. And it's significant, Jessica. Never forget that. You may think you have one foot in the poorhouse, but Crosslyn Rise, for all its problems, is worth a pretty penny. It'll be worth even more once it's developed."

Developed. The word made her flinch. She felt guilty for even considering it—guilty, traitorous, mercenary. In one instant she was disappointed with herself, in the next she was furious with her father.

But neither disappointment nor fury would change the facts. "Why does this have to be?" she whispered sadly.

"Because," Gordon said quietly, "life goes on. Things change." He tipped his head and eyed her askance. "It may not be all that bad. You must be lonely living at the Rise all by yourself. It's a pretty big place. You could choose one of the smaller houses and have it custom-designed for you."

She held up a cautionary hand. He was moving a little too quickly. "I haven't decided to do this."

"It's a solid idea."

"But you're making it sound as if it can really happen, and that makes me feel like I'm losing control."

"You'd be a member of the consortium," he reminded her. "You'd have a voice as to what's done."

"I'd be one out of three or six or maybe even twelve."

"But you own the Rise. In the end, you'd have final approval of any plan that is devised."

"I would?"

"Yes."

That made her feel better, but only a little. She'd always been an introverted sort. She could just imagine herself sitting at the far end of a table, listening to a group of glib investors bicker over her future. She'd be outtalked, outplanned, outwitted.

"I want more than that," she said on impulse. It was survivalism at its best. "I want to head the consortium. I want my cut to be the largest. I want to be *guaranteed* control over the end result." She straightened in her chair. "Is that possible?"

Gordon's brows rose. "Anything's possible. But advisable? I don't know, Jessica. You're a scholar. You don't know anything about real estate development."

"So I'll listen and learn. I have common sense and an artistic eye. I know the kind of thing I want. And I love Crosslyn Rise." She was convincing herself as she talked. "It isn't enough for me to have the power to approve or disapprove. I want to be part of the project from start to finish. That's the only way I'll be able to sleep at night." She wasn't sure she liked the look on Gordon's face. "You don't think I can do it."

"It's not that." He hesitated. There were several problems that he could see, one of which was immediate. He searched for the words to tell her what he was thinking, without sounding offensive. "You have to understand, Jessica. Traditionally, men are the investors. They've been involved in other projects. They're used to working in certain ways. I'm...not sure how they'll feel about a novice telling them what to do."

"A woman, you mean," she said, and he didn't deny it. "But I'm a reasonable person. I'm not pigheaded or spiteful. I'll be open-minded about everything except compromising the dignity of Crosslyn Rise. What better a leader could they want?"

Gordon didn't want to touch that one. So he tried a different tack. "Changing the face of Crosslyn Rise is going to be painful for you. Are you sure you want to be intimately involved in the process?"

"Yes," she declared.

He pursed his lips, dropped his gaze to the desktop, tried to think of other evasive arguments, but failed. Finally he went with the truth, bluntly stating the crux of the problem. "The fact is, Jessica, that if you insist on being the active head of the consortium, I may have trouble getting investors." He held up a hand. "Nothing personal, mind you. Most of the people I have in mind don't know who or what you are, but the fact of a young, inexperienced woman having such control over the project may make them skittish. They'll fear that it will take forever to make decisions, or that once those decisions are made, you'll change your mind. It goes back to the issue of credibility."

"That's not fair!"

"Life isn't, sometimes," he murmured, but he had an idea. "There is one way we might be able to get around it."

"What?"

He was thoughtful for another minute. "A compromise, sort of. We get the entire idea down on paper first. You work with an architect, tell him what you want, let him come up with some sketches, work with him on revising them until you're completely satisfied. Then we approach potential investors with a fait accompli." He was warming to the idea as he talked. "It could work out well. With your ideas spelled out in an architect's plans, we can better calculate the costs. Being specific might help in wooing investors."

"You mean, counterbalance the handicap of working with me?" Jessica suggested dryly, but she wasn't angry. If sexism existed, it existed. She had worked around it before. She could do it again.

"Things would be simplified all around," Gordon went on without comment. "You would have total control over the design of the project. Investors would know exactly what they were buying into. If they don't like your idea, they don't have to invest, and if we can't get enough people together, you'd only be out the architect's fee."

"How much will that be?" Jessica asked. She'd heard complaints from a colleague who had worked with an architect not long before.

"Not as much as it might be, given the man I have in mind."

Jessica wasn't sure whether to be impressed or nervous. The bravado she's felt moments before was beginning to falter with talk of specifics, like architects. "You've already thought of someone?"

"Yes," Gordon said, eyeing her directly. "He's the best, and Crosslyn Rise deserves the best."

She couldn't argue with that. "Who is he?"

"He's only been in the field for twelve years, but he's done some incredible things. He was affiliated with a New York firm for seven of those years, and during that time he worked on PUDs up and down the East Coast."

"PUDs?"

"Planned Urban Developments—in and around cities, out to suburbs. Five years ago, he established his own firm in Boston. He's done projects like the one you have in mind. I've seen them. They're breathtaking."

Her curiosity was piqued. "Who is he?"

"He's a down-to-earth guy who's had hands-on experience at the building end, which makes him an even better architect. He isn't so full of himself that he's hard to work with. And I think he'd be very interested in this project."

Jessica was trying to remember whether she'd ever read anything in the newspaper about an architect who might fit Gordon's description. But such an article would have been in the business section, and she didn't read that— which, unfortunately, underscored some of what Gordon had said earlier. Still, she had confidence in her ideas. And if she was to work with a man the likes of whom Gordon was describing, she couldn't miss.

"Who *is* he?" she asked.

"Carter Malloy."

Jessica stared at him dumbly. The name was very familiar. Carter Malloy. She frowned. Bits and snatches of memories began flitting through her mind.

"I knew a Carter Malloy once," she mused. "He was the son of the people who used to work for us at the Rise. His mom kept the house and his dad gardened." She felt a moment's wistfulness. "Boy, could I ever use Michael Malloy's green thumb now. On top of everything else, the Rise needs a landscaping overhaul. It's been nearly ten years since the Malloys retired and went south." Her wistfulness faded, giving way to a scowl. "It's been even longer since I've seen their son, thank goodness. He was obnoxious. He was older than me and never let me forget it. It used to drive him nuts that his parents were poor and mine weren't. He had a foul mouth, problems in school and a chip on his shoulder a mile wide. And he was ugly."

Gordon's expression was guarded, his voice low. "He's not ugly now."

"Excuse me?"

"I said," he repeated more clearly, "he's not ugly now. He's grown up in lots of ways, including that."

Jessica was surprised. "You've been in touch with Carter Malloy?"

"He keeps an account here. God only knows he could easily give his business to one of the bigger banks in Boston, but he says he feels a connection with the place where he grew up."

"No doubt he does. There's a little thing about a police record here. Petty theft, wasn't it?"

"He's reformed."

Her expression said she doubted that was possible. "I was always mystified that wonderful people like Annie and Michael Malloy could spawn a son like that. The heartache he caused them." She shook her head at the shame of it. "He's not living around her, is he? Tell me, so I'll know to watch out. Carter Malloy isn't someone I'd want to bump into on the street."

"He's living in Boston."

"What is he—a used-car salesman?"

"He's an architect."

Jessica was momentarily taken aback. "Not the Carter Malloy I knew."

"Like I said, he's grown up."

The thought that popped into her head at that moment was so horrendous that she quickly dashed it from mind. "The Carter Malloy I knew couldn't possibly have grown up to be a professional. He barely finished high school."

"He spent time in the army and went to college when he got out."

"But even if he had the gray matter for college," she argued, feeling distinctly uneasy, "he didn't have the patience or the dedication. He could never apply himself to anything for long. The only thing he succeeded at was making trouble."

"People change, Jessica. Carter Malloy is now a well-respected and successful architect."

Jessica had never known Gordon to lie to her, which was why she had to accept what he said. On a single lingering thread of hope, she gave a tight laugh. "Isn't it a coincidence? Two Carter Malloys, both architects? The one you have in mind for my project—does he live in Boston, too, or does he have a house in one of the suburbs?"

Gordon never answered. Jessica took one look at his expression, stood and began to pace the office. Her hands were tucked into the pockets of her skirt, and just as the challis fabric faithfully rendered the slenderness of her hips and legs as she paced, it showed those hands balled into fists. Her arms were straight, pressed to her sides.

"Do you know what Carter Malloy did to me when I was six? He dared me to climb to the third notch of the big elm out beyond the duck pond." She turned at the window and stared back. "Needless to say, once I got up there, I couldn't get back down. He looked up at me with that pimply face of his, gave an evil grin and walked off." She paused before a Currier and Ives print on the wall, seeing nothing of it. "I was terrified. I sat for a while thinking that he'd come back, but he didn't. I tried yelling, but I was too far from the house to be heard. One hour passed, then another, and each time I looked at the ground I got dizzy. I sat up there crying for three hours before Michael finally found me, and then he had to call the fire department to get me down." She moved on. "I had nightmares for weeks afterward. I've never climbed a tree since."

She stopped at the credenza, turned and faced Gordon, dropping her hands and hips back against the polished mahogany for support. "If the Carter Malloy I knew is the one you have in mind for this job, the answer is no. That's my very first decision as head of this consortium, and it's closed to discussion."

"Now that," Gordon said on a light note that wasn't light at all but was his best shot at an appeal, "is why I may have trouble finding backers for the project. If you're going to make major decisions without benefit of discussion with those who have more experience, there isn't much hope. I have to say that I wouldn't put my money into a venture like that. A bullheaded woman would be hell to work with."

"Gordon," she protested.

"I'm serious, Jessica. You said you'd listen and learn, but you don't seem willing to do that."

"I am. Just not where Carter Malloy is concerned. I couldn't work with him. It would be a disaster, and what would happen to the Rise, then?" Her voice grew pleading. "There must be other architects. He can't be the only one available."

"He's not, and there are others, but he's the best."

"In all of Boston?"

"Given the circumstances, yes."

"What circumstances?"

"He knows the Rise. He cares about it."

"Cares?" she echoed in dismay. "He'd as soon burn the Rise to the ground and leave it in ashes as transform it into something beautiful."

"How do you know? When was the last time you talked with him?"

"When I was sixteen." Pushing off from the credenza, she began to pace again. "It was the first I'd seen him in a while—"

"He'd been in the army," Gordon interrupted to remind her.

"Whatever. His parents didn't talk about him much, and I was the last person who'd want to ask. But he came over to get something for his dad one night. I was on the front porch waiting for a date to pick me up, and Carter said—" Her memories interrupted her this time. Their sting held her silent for a minute, finally allowing her to murmur, "He said some cruel things. Hurtful things." She stopped her pacing to look at Gordon. "Carter Malloy hates me as much as I hate him. There's no way he'd agree to do the work for me even if I wanted him to do it, which I don't."

But Gordon wasn't budging. "He'd do it. And he'd do it well. The Carter Malloy I've come to know over the past five years is a very different man from the one you remember. Didn't you ever wonder why his parents retired when they did? They were in their late fifties, not terribly old and in no way infirm. But they'd saved a little money over the years, and then Carter bought them a place in Florida with beautiful shrubbery that Michael could tend year-round. It was one of the first things Carter did when he began to earn good money. To this day he sees that they have everything they need. It's his way of making up for the trouble he caused them when he was younger. If he hurt you once, my guess is he'd welcome the chance to help out now."

"I doubt that," she scoffed, but more quietly. She was surprised by what Gordon had said. Carter Malloy had never struck her as a man with a thoughtful bone in his body. "What do you mean by help out?"

"I'd wager that he'd join the consortium."

"Out of pity for me?"

"Not at all. He's a shrewd businessman. He'd join it for the investment value. But he'd also want to be involved for old times' sake. I've heard him speak fondly of Crosslyn Rise." He paused, stroked a finger over his upper lip. "I'd go so far as to say we could get him to throw in his fee as part of his contribution. That way, he'd have a real stake in making the plans work, and if they didn't, it would be his problem. He'd swallow his own costs—which would be a far sight better than your having to come up with forty or fifty thousand if the project fizzled."

"Forty or fifty thousand?" She hadn't dreamed it would be so much. Swallowing, she sank into her chair once again, this time into the deepest corner, where the chair's back and arms could shield her. "I don't like this, Gordon."

"I know. But given that the Rise can't be saved as it is, this is an exciting option. Let me call Carter."

"No," she cried, then repeated it more quietly. "No."

"I'm talking about a simple introductory meeting. You can tell him your general thoughts about the project and listen to what he has to say in return. See how you get along. Decide for yourself whether he's the same as he used to be. There won't be an obligation. I'll be there with you if you like."

She tipped up her chin. "I was never afraid of Carter Malloy. I just disliked him."

"You won't now. He's a nice guy. Y'know, you said it yourself—it drove him nuts that he was poor and you were rich. He must have spent a lot of time wishing Crosslyn Rise was his. So let him take those wishes and your ideas and make you some sketches."

"They could be very good or very bad."

"Ah," Gordon drawled, "but remember two things. First off, Carter has a career and a reputation to protect. Second, you have final say. If you don't like what he does, you have the power of veto. In a sense that puts him under your thumb, now, doesn't it?"

Jessica thought back to the last time she'd seen Carter Malloy. In vivid detail, she recalled what he'd said to her, and though she'd blotted it from her mind over the years, the hurt and humiliation remained. Perhaps she would find a measure of satisfaction having him under her thumb.

And, yes, Crosslyn Rise was still hers. If Carter Malloy didn't come up with plans that pleased her, she'd turn her back on him and walk away. He'd see who had the last laugh then.

2

JESSICA HAD NEVER BEEN a social butterfly. Her mother, well aware of the Crosslyn heritage, had put her through the motions when she'd been a child. Jessica had been dressed up and taken to birthday parties, given riding lessons, sent to summer camp, enrolled in ballet. She had learned the essentials of being a properly privileged young lady. But she had never quite fit in.

She wasn't a beautiful child, for one thing. Her hair was long and unruly, her body board-straight and her features plain—none of which was helped by the fact that she rarely smiled. She was quiet, serious, shy, not terribly unlike her father. One part of her was most comfortable staying home in her room at Crosslyn Rise reading a good book. The other part dreamed of being the belle of the ball.

Having a friend over to play was both an apprehensive and exciting experience for Jessica. She liked the company and, even more, the idea of being liked, but she was forever afraid of boring her guest. At least, that was what her mother warned her against ad infinitum. As an adult, Jessica understood that though her mother worshipped her father's intellect, deep inside she found him a boring person, hence the warnings to Jessica. At the time, Jessica took those warning to heart. When she had a friend at the Rise, she was on her guard to impress.

That was why she was crushed by what Carter Malloy did to her when she was ten. Laura Hamilton, who came as close to being a best friend as any Jessica had, was over to visit. She didn't come often; the Rise wasn't thought to be a "fun" place. But Laura had come this time because she and Jessica had a project to do together for school, and the library at the Rise had the encyclopedias and *National Geographics* that the girls needed.

When they finished their work, Jessica suggested they go out to the porch. It was a warm fall day, and the porch was one of her favorite spots. Screened in and heavily shaded by towering maples and oaks, it was the kind of quiet, private place that made Jessica feel secure.

She started out feeling secure this day, because Laura liked the porch, too. They sat close beside each other on the flowered porch sofa, pads of paper in their laps, pencils in hand. They were writing poems, which seemed to Jessica to be an exciting enough thing to do.

Carter Malloy didn't think so. Pruning sheers in hand, he materialized from behind the rhododendrons just beyond the screen, where, to Jessica's chagrin, he had apparently been sitting.

"What are you two doing?" he asked in a voice that said he knew exactly what they were doing, since he'd been listening for quite some time, and he thought it was totally dumb.

"What are *you* doing?" Jessica shot right back. She wasn't intimidated by his size or his deep voice or the fact that he was seventeen. Maybe, just a little, she was intimidated by his streetwise air, but she pushed that tiny fear aside. Given who his parents were, he wouldn't dare touch her. "What are you doing out there?" she demanded.

"Clipping the hedges," Carter answered with an insolent look.

She was used to the look. It put her on the defensive every time she saw it. "No, you weren't. You were spying on us."

He had one hip cocked, one shoulder lower than the other but both back to emphasize a developing chest. "Why in the hell would I want to do that? You're writing sissy poems."

"Who is he?" Laura whispered nervously.

"He's no one," was Jessica's clearly spoken answer. Though she'd always talked back to Carter, this time it seemed more important than ever. She had Laura to impress. "You were supposed to be cutting the shrubs, but you weren't. You never do what your father tells you to do."

"I think for myself," Carter answered. His dark eyes bore into hers. "But you don't know what that means. You're either going to tea parties like your old lady or sticking your nose in a book like your old man. You couldn't think for yourself if you tried. So whose idea was it to write poems? Your prissy little friend's?"

Jessica didn't know which to be first, angry or embarrassed. "Go away, Carter."

Lazily he raised the pruning sheers and snipped off a single shoot. "I'm working."

"Go work somewhere else," she cried with a ten-year-old's frustration. "There are lots of other bushes."

"But this one needs trimming."

She was determined to hold her ground. "We want to be alone."

"Why? What's so important about writing poems? Afraid I'll steal your rhymes?" He looked closely at Laura. "You're a Hamilton, aren't you?"

"Don't answer," Jessica told Laura.

"She is," Carter decided. "I've seen her sitting in church with the rest of her family."

"That's a lie," Jessica said. "You don't go to church."

"I go sometimes. It's fun, all those sinners begging for forgiveness. Take old man Hamilton. He bought his way into the state legislature—"

Jessica was on her feet, her reed-slim body shaking. The only thing she knew for sure about what Carter was saying was that it was certain to offend Laura, and if that happened, Laura would never be back. "Shut up, Carter!"

"Bought his way there and does nothing but sit on his can and raise his hand once in a while. But I s'pose he doesn't have to do nothing. If I had that much money, I'd be sittin' on my can, too."

"You *don't* have that much money. You don't have *any* money."

"But I have friends. And you don't."

Jessica never knew how he'd found her Achilles' heel, but he'd hit her where it hurt. "You're a stupid jerk," she cried. "You're dumb and you have pimples. I wouldn't want to be you for anything in the world." Tears swimming in her eyes, she took Laura's hand and dragged her into the house.

Laura never did come back to Crosslyn Rise, and looking back on it so many years later, Jessica remembered the hurt she'd felt. It didn't matter that she hadn't seen Laura Hamilton for years, that by the time they'd reached high school Jessica had found her as boring as she'd feared she would be herself, that they had nothing in common now. The fact was that when she was ten, she had badly wanted to be Laura's best friend and Carter Malloy had made that harder than ever.

Such were her thoughts as the *T* carried her underground from one stop to the next on her way from Harvard Square to Boston. She had a two-o'clock meeting with Carter Malloy in his office. Gordon had set it up, and when he'd asked if Jessica wanted him along, she had said she'd be fine on her own.

She wasn't sure that had been the wisest decision. She was feeling nervous, feeling as though every one of the insecurities she'd suffered in childhood was back in force. She was the not-too-pretty, not-too-popular, not-too-social little girl once again. Gordon's support might have come in handy.

But she had a point to prove to him, too. She'd told him that she wanted to actively head the consortium altering Crosslyn Rise. Gordon was skeptical of her ability to do that. If he was to aggressively and enthusiastically seek out investors in Crosslyn Rise, she had to show him she was up to the job.

So she'd assured him that she could handle Carter Malloy on her own, and that, she decided in a moment's respite from doubt, was what she was going to do. But the doubts returned, and as she left the trolley, climbed the steep stairs to Park Street and headed for Winter, she hated Carter Malloy more than ever.

It wasn't the best frame of mind in which to be approaching a meeting of some importance, Jessica knew, which was why she took a slight detour on her way to Carter's office. She had extra time; punctual person that she was, she'd allowed plenty for the ride from Cambridge. So she swung over to West Street and stopped to browse at the Brattle Book Shop, and though she didn't buy anything, the sense of comfort she felt in the company of books, particularly the aged beauties George Gloss had collected, was worth the pause. It was with some reluctance that she finally dragged herself away from the shelves and set off.

Coming from school, she wore her usual teaching outfit—long skirt, soft blouse, slouchy blazer and low heels.

The occasional glance in a store window as she passed told her that she looked perfectly presentable. Her hair was impossible, of course. Though not as unruly as it had once been, it was still thick and hard to handle, which was why she had it secured with a scarf at the back of her head. She wasn't trying to impress anyone, least of all Carter Malloy, but she wanted to look professional and in command of herself, if nothing else.

Carter's firm was on South Street in an area that had newly emerged as a mecca for artists and designers. The building itself was six stories tall and of an earthy brick that was a pleasantly warm in contrast to the larger, more modern office tower looming nearby. The street level of the building held a chic art gallery, an equally chic architectural supply store, a not-so-chic fortune cookie company, and a perfectly dumpy-looking diner that was mobbed, even at two, with a suit-and-tie crowd.

Turning in at the building's main entrance, she couldn't help but be impressed by the newly refurbished, granite-walled lobby. She guessed that the building's rents were high, attesting to Gordon's claim that Carter was doing quite well.

As she took the elevator to the top floor, Jessica struggled, as she'd done often in the five days since Gordon had first mentioned his name, to reconcile the Carter Malloy she'd known with the Carter Malloy who was a successful architect. Try as she might, she couldn't shake the image of what he'd been as a boy and what he'd done to her then. Not even the sleekly modern reception area, with its bright walls, indirect lighting and sparse, avante-garde furnishings could displace the image of the ill-tempered, sleezy-looking juvenile delinquent.

"My name is Jessica Crosslyn," she told the receptionist in a voice that was quiet and didn't betray the unease she felt. "I have a two-o'clock appointment with Mr. Malloy."

The receptionist was an attractive woman, sleek enough to complement her surroundings, though nowhere near as new. Jessica guessed her to be in her late forties. "Won't you have a seat? Mr. Malloy was delayed at a meeting. He shouldn't be more than five or ten minutes. He's on his way now."

Jessica should have figured he'd be late. Keeping her waiting was a petty play for power. She was sure he'd planned it.

Once again she wished Gordon was with her, if for no other reason than to show him that Carter hadn't changed so much. But Gordon was up on the North Shore, and she was too uncomfortable to sit. So, nodding at the receptionist, she moved away from the desk and slowly passed one, then another of the large, dry-mounted drawings that hung on the wall. Hingham Court, Pheasant Landing, Berkshire Run—pretty names for what she had to admit were attractive complexes, if the drawings were at all true to life. If she could blot out the firm's name, Malloy and Goodwin, from the corner of each, she might feel enthusiasm. But the Malloy, in particular, kept jumping right off the paper, hitting her mockingly in the face. In self-defense, she finally turned and slipped into one of the low armchairs.

Seconds later, the door opened and her heart began to thud. Four men entered, engaged in a conversation that kept them fully occupied while her gaze went from one face to the next. Gordon had said Carter Malloy had changed a lot, but even accounting for that, not one of the men remotely resembled the man she remembered.

Feeling awkward, she took a magazine from the glass coffee table beside her and began to leaf through. She figured that if Carter was in the group, he'd know of her presence soon enough. In the meanwhile, she concentrated on keeping her glasses straight on her nose and looking calm, cool, even a bit disinterested, which was hard when the discussion among the four men began to grow heated. The matter at hand seemed to be the linkage issue, a City of Boston mandate that was apparently costing builders hundreds of thousands of dollars per project. Against her will, she found herself looking up. One of the group seemed to be with the city, another with Carter's firm and the other two with a construction company. She was thinking that the architect was the most articulate of the bunch when the door opened again. Her heart barely had time to start pounding anew when Carter Malloy came through. He took in the group before him, shook hands with the three she'd pegged as outsiders, slid a questioning gaze to the receptionist, then, in response to the woman's pointed glance, looked at Jessica.

For the space of several seconds, her heart came to a total standstill. The man was unmistakably Carter Malloy, but, yes, he'd changed. He was taller, broader. In place of a sweaty T-shirt emblazoned with something obscene, tattered old jeans and crusty work boots, he wore a tweed blazer, an oxford-cloth shirt with the neck button open, gray slacks and loafers. The dark hair that had always fallen in ungroomed spikes on his forehead was shorter, well shaped, cleaner. His skin, too, was cleaner, his features etched by time. The surly expression that even now taunted her memory had mellowed to something still intense but controlled. He had tiny lines shadowing the corners of his eyes, a small scar on his right jaw and a light tan.

Gordon was right, she realized in dismay. Carter wasn't ugly anymore. He wasn't *at all* ugly, and that complicated things. She didn't do well with men in general, but attractive ones in particular made her edgy. She wasn't sure she was going to make it.

But she couldn't run out now. That would be the greatest indignity. And besides, if she did that, what would she tell Gordon? More aptly, what would Carter tell Gordon? Her project would be sunk, for sure.

Mustering every last bit of composure she had stashed away inside, she rose as Carter approached.

"Jessica?" he asked in a deep but tentative voice.

Heart thudding, she nodded. She deliberately kept her hands in her lap. To offer a handshake seemed reckless.

Fortunately he didn't force the issue, but stood looking down at her, not quite smiling, not quite frowning. "I'm sorry. Were you waiting long?"

She shook her head. A little voice inside told her to say something, but for the life of her she couldn't find any words. She was wondering why she felt so small, why Carter seemed so tall, how her memory could have been so inaccurate in its rendition of as simple a matter as relative size.

He gestured toward the inner door. "Shall we go inside?"

She nodded. When he opened the door and held it for her, she was surprised; the Carter she'd known would have let it slam in her face. When she felt the light pressure of his hand at her waist, guiding her down a corridor spattered with offices, she was doubly surprised; the Carter she'd known knew nothing of courtly gestures, much less gentleness. When he said, "Here we are," and showed her into the farthest and largest office, she couldn't help but be impressed.

That feeling lasted for only a minute, because no sooner had she taken a chair—gratefully, since the race of her pulse was making her legs shaky—than Carter backed himself against the stool that stood at the nearby drafting table, looked at her with a familiarly wicked gleam in his eye and said, "Cat got your tongue?"

Jessica was oddly relieved. The old Carter Malloy she could handle to some extent; sarcasm was less debilitating than charm. Taking in a full breath for the first time since she'd laid eyes on him, she said, "My tongue's where it's always been. I don't believe in using it unless I have something to say."

"Then you're missing out on some of the finer things in life," he informed her so innocently that it was a minute before Jessica connected his words with the gleam in his eye.

Ignoring both the innuendo and the faint flush that rose on her cheeks, she vowed to state her business as quickly as possible and leave. "Did Gordon explain why I've come?"

Carter gave a leisurely nod, showing none of the discomfort she felt. But instead of picking up on his conversation with Gordon, he said, "It's been a long time. How have you been?"

"Just fine."

"You're looking well."

She wasn't sure why he'd said that, but it annoyed her. "I haven't changed," she told him as though stating the obvious, then paused. "You have."

"I should hope so." While the words settled into the stillness of the room, he continued to stare at her. His eyes were dark, touched one minute by mockery, the next by genuine curiosity. Jessica half wished for the contempt she used to find there. It wouldn't have been as unsettling.

Tearing her gaze from his, she looked down at her hands, used one to shove the nose piece of her glasses higher and cleared her throat. "I've decided to make some changes at Crosslyn Rise." She looked back up, but before she could say a thing, Carter beat her to it.

"I'm sorry about your father's death."

Uh-huh, she thought, but she simply nodded in thanks for the words. "Anyway, there's only me now, so the Rise is really going to waste." That wasn't the issue at all, but she couldn't quite get herself to tell Carter Malloy the problem was money. "I'm hoping to make something newer and more practical out of it. Gordon suggested I speak with you. Quite honestly, I wasn't wild about the idea." She watched him closely, waiting to see his reaction to her rebuff.

But he gave nothing away. In a maddeningly calm voice, he asked, "Why not?"

She didn't blink. "We never liked one another. Working together could be difficult."

"That's assuming we don't like one another now," he pointed out too reasonably.

"We don't *know* one another now."

"Which is why you're here today."

"Yes," she said, hesitated, then added, "I wasn't sure how much to believe of what Gordon told me." Her eyes roamed the room, taking in a large desk covered with rolls of blueprints, the drafting table and its tools, a corked wall that bore sketches in various stages of completion. "All this doesn't jibe with the man I remember."

"That man wasn't a man. He wasn't much more than a boy. How many years has it been since we last saw each other?"

"Seventeen," she said quickly, then wished she'd been slower or more vague when she caught a moment's satisfaction in his eye.

"You didn't know I was an architect?"

"How would I know?"

He shrugged and offered a bit too innocently, "Mutual friends?"

She did say, "Uh-huh," aloud this time, and with every bit of the sarcasm she'd put into it before. He was obviously enjoying her discomfort. *That* was more like what she'd expected. "We've never had any mutual friends."

"Spoken like the Jessica I remember, arrogant to the core. But times have changed, sweetheart. I've come up in the world. For starters, there's Gordon. He's a mutual friend."

"And he'd have had no more reason to keep me apprised of your comings and goings than I'd have had to ask. The last I knew of you," she said, her voice hard in anger that he'd dared call her 'sweetheart,' "you were stealing cars."

Carter's indulgent expression faded, replaced by something with a sharper edge. "I made some mistakes when I was younger, and I paid the price. I had to start from the bottom and work my way up. I didn't have any help, but I made it."

"And how many people did you hurt along the way?"

"None once I got going, too many before," he admitted. His face was somber, and though his body kept the same pose, the relaxation had left it. "I burned a whole lot of bridges that I've had to rebuild. That was one of the reasons I shifted my schedule to see you when Gordon called. You were pretty bitchy when you were a kid, but I fed into it."

She stiffened. "Bitchy? Thanks a lot!"

"I said I fed into it. I'm willing to take most of the blame, but you were bitchy. Admit it. Your hackles went up whenever you saw me."

"Do you wonder why? You said and did the nastiest things to me. It got so I was conditioned to expect it. I did whatever I could to protect myself, and that meant being on my guard at the first sight of you."

Rather than argue further, he pushed off from the stool and went to the desk. He stood at its side, fingering a paper clip for a minute before meeting her gaze again. "My parents send their best."

Jessica was nearly as surprised by the gentling of his voice as she was by what he'd said. "You told them we were meeting?"

"I talked with them last night." At the look of disbelief that remained on her face, he said, "I do that sometimes."

"You never used to. You were horrible to them, too."

Carter returned his attention to the paper clip, which he twisted and turned with the fingers of one hand. "I know."

"But why? They were wonderful people. I used to wish my parents were half as easygoing and good-natured as yours. And you treated them so badly."

He shot her a look of warning. "It's easy to think someone else's parents are wonderful when you're the one who doesn't live with them. You don't know the facts, Jessica. My relationship with my parents was very complex." He paused for a deep breath, which seemed to restore his good temper. "Anyway, they want to know everything about you—how you look, whether you're working or married or mothering, how the Rise is."

The last thing Jessica wanted to do was to discuss her personal life with Carter. He would be sure to tear it apart and make her feel more inadequate than ever. So she blurted out, "I'll tell you how the Rise is. It's big and beautiful, but it's aging. Either I pour a huge amount of money into renovations, or I make alternate plans. That's why I'm here. I want to discuss the alternate plans."

Carter made several more turns of the paper clip between his fingers before he tossed it aside. Settling his tall frame into the executive chair behind the desk, he folded his hands over his lean middle and said quietly, "I'm listening."

Business, this is business, Jessica told herself and took strength from the thought. "I don't know how much Gordon has told you, but I'm thinking of turning Crosslyn Rise into a condominium complex, building cluster housing in the woods, turning the mansion into a common facility for the owners, putting a marina along the shore."

Gordon hadn't told Carter much of anything, judging from the look of disbelief on his face. "Why would you do that?"

"Because the Rise is too big for me."

"So find someone it isn't too big for."

"I've been trying to, but the market's terrible."

"It takes a while sometimes to find the right buyer."

I don't have a while, she thought. "It could take years, and I'd really like to do something before then."

"Is there a rush? Crosslyn Rise has been in your family for generations. A few more years is nothing in the overall scheme of things."

Jessica wished he wouldn't argue. She didn't like what she was saying much more than he did. "I think it's time to make a change."

"But condominiums?" he asked in dismay. "Why condominiums?"

"Because the alternative is a full-fledged housing development, and that would be worse. This way, at least, I'd have some control over the outcome."

"Why does that have to be the alternative?"

"Do you have any better ideas?" she asked dryly.

"Sure. If you can't find an individual, sell to an institution—a school or something like that."

"No institution, or school or something like that will take care of the Rise the right way. I can just picture large parking lots and litter all over the place."

"Then what about the town? Deed the Rise to the town for use as a museum. Just imagine the whopping big tax deduction you'd get."

"I'm not looking for tax deductions, and besides, the town may be wealthy, but it isn't *that* wealthy. Do you have any idea what the costs are of maintaining Crosslyn Rise for a year?" Realizing she was close to giving herself away, she paused and said more calmly, "In the end, the town would have to sell it, and I'd long since have lost my say."

"But . . . condominiums?"

"Why not?" she sparred, hating him for putting her on the spot when, if he had any sensitivity at all, he'd know she was between a rock and a very hard place.

Carter leaned forward in his seat and pinned her with a dark-eyed stare. "Because Crosslyn Rise is magnificent. It's one of the most beautiful, most private, most special pieces of property I've ever seen, and believe me, I've seen a whole lot in the last few years. I don't even know how you can think of selling it."

"I have no choice!" she cried, and something in her eyes must have told him the truth.

"You can't keep it up?"

She dropped her gaze to the arm of her chair and rubbed her thumb back and forth against the chrome. "That's right." Her voice was quiet, imbued with the same defeat it had held in Gordon's office, and with an additional element of humiliation. Admitting the truth was bad enough; admitting it to Carter Malloy was even worse.

But she had to finish what she'd begun. "Like I said, the Rise is aging. Work that should have been done over the years wasn't, so what needs to be done now is extensive."

"Your dad let it go."

She had an easier time not looking at him. At least his voice was kind. "Not intentionally. But his mind was elsewhere, and my mother didn't want to upset him. Money was—" She stopped herself, realizing in one instant that she didn't want to make the confession, knowing in the next that she had to. "Money was tight."

"Are you kidding?"

Meeting his incredulous gaze, she said coldly, "No. I wouldn't kid about something like that."

"You don't kid about much of anything. You never did. Afraid a smile might crack your face?"

Jessica stared at him for a full second. "You haven't changed a bit," she muttered, and rose from her chair. "I shouldn't have come here. It was a mistake. I knew it would be."

She was just about at the door when it closed and Carter materialized before her. "Don't go," he said very quietly. "I'm sorry if I offended you. I sometimes say things without thinking them through. I've been working on improving that. I guess I still have a ways to go."

The thing that appalled Jessica most at that minute wasn't the embarrassment she felt regarding the Rise or her outburst or even Carter's apology. It was how handsome he was. Her eyes held his for a moment before, quite helplessly, lowering over the shadowed angle of his jaw to his chin, then his mouth. His lower lip was fuller than the top one. The two were slightly parted, touched only by the air he breathed.

Wrenching her gaze to the side, she swallowed hard and hung her head. "I do think this is a mistake," she murmured. "The whole thing is very difficult for me. Working with you won't help that."

"But I care about Crosslyn Rise."

"That was what Gordon said. But maybe you care most about getting it away from me. You always resented me for the Rise."

The denial she might have expected never came. After a short time, he said, "I resented lots of people for things that I didn't have. I was wrong. I'm not saying that I wouldn't buy the Rise from you if I had the money, because I meant what I said about it being special. But I don't have the money—any more, I guess, than you do. So that puts us in the same boat. On equal footing. Neither of us above or below the other."

He paused, giving her a chance to argue, but she didn't have anything to say. He had a right to be smug, she knew, but at that moment he wasn't. He was being completely reasonable.

"Do you have trouble with that, Jessica? Can you regard me as an equal?"

"We're not at all alike, you and I."

"I didn't say alike. I said equal. I meant financially equal."

Keeping her eyes downcast, she cocked her head toward the office behind her. "Looks to me like you're doing a sight better than I am at this point."

"But you have the Rise. That's worth a lot." When she simply shrugged, he said, "Sit down. Please. Let's talk."

Jessica wasn't quite sure why she listened to him. She figured it had something to do with the gentle way he'd asked, with the word "please," with the fact that he was blocking the door anyway, and he wasn't a movable presence. She suspected it might have even had something to do with her own curiosity. Though she caught definite reminders of the old Carter, the changes that had taken place since she'd seen him last intrigued her.

Without a word, she returned to her seat. This time, rather than going behind his desk, Carter lowered his long frame into the matching chair next to hers. Though there was a low slate cube between them, he was closer, more visible. That made her feel self-conscious. To counter the feeling, she directed her eyes to her hands and her thoughts to the plans she wanted to make for Crosslyn Rise.

"I don't like the sound of condominiums, either, but if the condominiums were in the form of cluster housing, if they were well placed and limited in number, if the renovations to the mansion were done with class and the waterfront likewise, the final product wouldn't be so bad. At least it would be kept up. The owners would be paying a lot for the privilege of living there. They'd have a stake in its future."

"Are you still teaching?"

At the abrupt change of subject, she cast him a quick look. "I, uh, yes."

"You haven't remarried?"

When her eyes flew to his this time, they stayed. "How did you know I'd married at all?"

"My parents. They were in touch with your mom. Once she died, they lost contact."

"Dad isn't—wasn't very social," Jessica said by way of explanation. But she hadn't kept in touch with the Malloys, either. "I'm not much better, I guess. How have your parents been?"

"Very well," he said on the lightest note he'd used yet. "They really like life under the sun. The warm weather is good for Mom's arthritis, and Dad is thrilled with the long growing season."

"Do you see them often?"

"Three or four times a year. I've been pretty busy."

She pressed her lips together and shook her head. "An architect. I'm still having trouble with that."

"What would you have me be?"

"A pool shark. A gambler. An ex-con."

He had the grace to look humble. "I suppose I deserved that."

"Yes." She was still looking at him, bound by something she couldn't quite fathom. She kept thinking that if she pushed a certain button, said a certain word, he'd change back into the shaggy-haired demon he'd been. But he wasn't changing into anything. He was just sitting with one leg crossed over the other, studying her intently. It was all she could do not to squirm. She averted her eyes, then, annoyed, returned them to his. "Why are you doing that?"

"Doing what?"

"Staring at me like that."

"Because you look different. I'm trying to decide how."

"I'm older. That's all."

"Maybe," he conceded, but said no more.

The silence chipped at Jessica's already-iffy composure nearly as much as his continued scrutiny did. She wasn't sure why she was the one on the hot seat, when by rights the hot seat should have been his. In an attempt to correct the situation, she said, "Since I have an appointment back in Cambridge at four—" which she'd deliberately planned, to give her an out "—I think we should concentrate on business. Gordon said you were good." She sent a look toward the corked wall. "Are these your sketches, or were they done by an assistant?"

"They're mine."

"And the ones in the reception area?"

"Some are mine, some aren't."

"Who is Goodwin?"

"My partner. We first met in New York. He specializes in commercial work. I specialize in residential, so we complement each other."

"Was he one of the men standing out front?"

"No. The man in the tan blazer was one of three associates who work here."

"What do they do—the associates?"

"They serve as project managers."

"Are they architects?" She could have sworn the man she'd heard talking was one.

Carter nodded. "Two are registered, the third is about to be. Beneath the associates, there are four draftspeople, beneath them a secretary, a bookkeeper and a receptionist."

"Are you the leading partner?"

"You mean, of the two of us, do I bring in more money?" When she nodded, he said, "I did last year. The year before I didn't. It varies."

"Would you want to work on Crosslyn Rise?"

"Not particularly," he stated, then held up a hand in appeasement when she looked angry. "I'd rather see the Rise kept as it is. If you want honesty, there it is. But if you don't have the money to support it, something has to be done." He came forward to brace his elbows on his thighs and dangle his hands between his knees. "And if you're determined to go ahead with the condo idea, I'd rather do the work myself than have a stranger do it."

"You're a stranger," she said stiffly. "You're not the same person who grew up around Crosslyn Rise."

"I remember what I felt for the Rise then. I can even better understand those feelings now."

"I'm not sure I trust your motives."

"Would I risk all this—" he shot a glance around the room "—for the sake of a vendetta? Look, Jessica," he said with a sigh, "I don't deny who I was then and what I did. I've already said that. I was a pain in the butt."

"You were worse than that."

"Okay, I was worse than that, but I'm a different person now. I've been through a whole lot that you can't begin to imagine. I've lived through hell and come out on the other side, and because of that, I appreciate some things other people don't. Crosslyn Rise is one of those things."

Jessica wished he wasn't sitting so close or regarding her so intently or talking so sanely. Either he was being utterly sincere, or he was doing one hell of an acting job. She wasn't sure which, but she did know that she couldn't summarily rule him off the project.

"Do you think," she asked in a tentative voice, "that my idea for Crosslyn Rise would work?"

"It could."

"Would you want to try working up some sketches?"

"We'd have to talk more about what you want. I'd need to see a plot plan. And I'd have to go out there. Even aside from the fact that I haven't been there in a while, I've never looked around with this kind of thing in mind."

Jessica nodded. What he said was fair enough. What wasn't fair was the smooth way he said it. He sounded very professional and very male. For the second time in as many minutes, she wished he wasn't sitting so close. She wished she wasn't so aware of him.

Clutching her purse, she stood. "I have to be going," she said, concentrating on the leather strap as she eased it over her shoulder.

"But we haven't settled anything."

She raised her eyes. He, too, had risen and was standing within an arm's length of her. She started toward the door. "We have. We've settled that we have to talk more, I have to get you a plot plan, you have to come out to see

Crosslyn Rise." Her eyes were on the doorknob, but she felt Carter moving right along with her. "You may want to talk with Gordon, too. He'll explain the plan he has for raising the money for the project."

"Am I hired?" He reached around her to open the door.

"I don't know. We have to do all those other things first."

"When can we meet again?"

"I'll call you." She was in the corridor, moving steadily back the way she'd come, with Carter matching her step.

"Why don't we set a time now?"

"Because I don't have my schedule in front of me."

"Are you that busy?"

"Yes!" she said, and stopped in her tracks. She looked up at him, swallowed tightly, dropped her gaze again and moved on. "Yes," she echoed in a near-whisper. "It's nearly exam time. My schedule's erratic during exam time."

Her explanation seemed to appease Carter, which relieved her, as did the sight of the reception area. She was feeling overwhelmed by Carter's presence. He was a little too smooth, a little too agreeable, a little too male. Between those things and a memory that haunted her, she wanted out.

"Will you call me?" he asked as he opened the door to the reception area.

"I said I would."

"You have my number?"

"Yes."

Opening the outer door, he accompanied her right to the elevator and pushed the button. "Can I have yours?"

Grateful for something to do, she fumbled in her purse for a pen, jotted her number in a small notebook, tore out the page and handed it to him. She was restowing the pen when a bell rang announcing the elevator's arrival. Her attention was riveted to the panel on top of the doors when Carter said, "Jessica?"

She dared meet his gaze a final time. It was a mistake. A small frown touched his brow and was gone, leaving an expression that combined confusion and surprise with pleasure. When he spoke, his voice held the same three elements. "It was really good seeing you," he said as though he meant it and surprised himself in that. Then he smiled, and his smile held nothing but pleasure.

That was when Jessica knew she was in big trouble.

3

CARTER *HAD* ENJOYED SEEING Jessica, though he wasn't sure why. As a kid, she'd been a snotty little thing looking down her nose at him. He had resented everything about her, which was why his greatest joy had been putting her down. In that, he had been cruel at times. He'd found her sore spots and rubbed them with salt.

Clearly she remembered. She wasn't any too happy to see him, though she'd agreed to the meeting, which said something about the bind she was in regarding Crosslyn Rise. Puzzled by that bind, Carter called Gordon shortly after Jessica left his office.

In setting up the meeting, Gordon had only told him that Jessica had wanted to discuss an architectural project relating to the Rise. Under Carter's questioning now, he admitted to the financial problems. He talked of putting together a group of investors. He touched on Jessica's insistence on being in command. He went so far as to outline the role Carter might play, as Gordon had broached it with Jessica.

Though Carter had meant what he'd said about preferring to leave Crosslyn Rise as it was, once he accepted the idea of its changing, he found satisfaction in the idea of taking part in that change. Some of his satisfaction was smug; there was an element of poetic justice in his having come far enough in the world to actively shape the Rise's future.

But the satisfaction went beyond that. Monetarily it was a sound proposal. His gut told him that, even before he worked out the figures. Given the dollar equivalent of his professional fees added to the hundred thousand he could afford to invest, he stood to take a sizable sum out of the project in two to three years' time.

That sum would go a long way toward broadening his base of operation. Malloy and Goodwin was doing well, bringing in greater profit each year, but there were certain projects—more artistically rewarding than lucrative—that Carter would bid on given the cushion of capital funds and a larger staff.

And then, working on the alteration of Crosslyn Rise both as architect and investor, he would see more of Jessica. That thought lingered with him long after he'd hung up the phone, long after he'd set aside the other issues.

He wanted to see more of her, incredible but true. She wasn't gorgeous. She wasn't sexy or witty. She wasn't anything like the women he dated, and it certainly wasn't that he was thinking of dating *her*. But at the end of their brief meeting, he had felt something warm flowing through him. He guessed it had to do with a shared past; he didn't have that with many people, and he wouldn't have thought he'd want it with *anyone*, given the sins of his past. Still, there was that warm feeling. It fascinated him, particularly since he had felt so many conflicting things during the meeting itself.

Emotions had come in flashes—anger and resentment in an almost automatic response to any hint of arrogance on her part, embarrassment and remorse as he recalled things he'd said and done years before. She was the same as he remembered her, but different—older, though time had been kind. Her skin was unflawed, her hair more tame, her movements more coordinated, even in spite of her nervousness. And she was nervous. He made her so, he guessed, though he had tried to be amenable.

What he wanted, he realized, was for her to eye him through those granny glasses of hers and see the decent person he was now. He wanted to close the last page on the book from the past. He wanted her acceptance. Though he hadn't given two thoughts to it before their meeting, that acceptance suddenly mattered a lot. Only when he had it would he feel that he'd truly conquered the past.

JESSICA TRIED TO THINK about their meeting as little as possible in the hours subsequent to it. To that end, she kept herself busy, which wasn't difficult with exams on the horizon and the resultant rash of impromptu meetings with students and teaching assistants. If Carter's phone number seemed to burn a hole in her date book, she ignored the smoke. She had to be in command, she told herself. Carter had to know she was in command.

She wasn't terribly proud of the show she'd put on in his office. She'd been skittish in his presence, and it had showed. The most merciful thing about the meeting was that he had waited until she had a foot out the door before smiling. His smile was potent. It had confused her, excited her, frightened her. It had warned her that working with him wasn't going to be easy in any way, shape or form, and it had nearly convinced her not to try it.

Still she called him. She waited two full days to do it, then chose Thursday afternoon, when she was fresh from a buoying department meeting. She enjoyed department meetings. She liked her colleagues and was liked in return. In the academic sphere, she was fully confident of her abilities. So she let the overflow of that confidence carry her into the phone call to Carter.

"Carter? This is Jessica Crosslyn."

"It's about time you called," he scolded, and she immediately bristled—until the teasing in his voice came through. "I was beginning to think you'd changed your mind."

She didn't know what to make of the teasing. She'd never heard teasing coming from Carter Malloy before. For the sake of their working together, she took it at face value and said evenly, "It's only been two days."

"That's two days too long."

"Is there a rush?"

"There's always a rush where enthusiasm and weather are concerned."

She found that to be a curious statement. "Enthusiasm?"

"I'm really up for this now, and I have the time to get started," he explained. "It's not often that the two coincide."

She could buy that, she supposed, though she wondered if he'd purposely injected the subtle reminder that he was in demand. "And the weather?" she came back a bit skeptically. "It's not yet May. The best of the construction season is still ahead."

"Not so, once time is spent on first-draft designs then multiple rounds of revisions." Carter kept his tone easygoing. "By the time the plans are done, the investors lined up and bidding taken on contractors, it could well be September or October, unless we step on it now." Having made his point, he paused. "Gordon explained the financial setup and the fact that you want sole approval of the final plans before they're shown to potential investors."

Jessica was immediately wary. "Do you have a problem with that?"

"It depends on whether you approve what I like," he said with a grin, then tacked on a quick, "Just kidding."

"I don't think you are."

"Sure I am," he cajoled. "A client pays me for my work, I give him what he wants."

"And if you think what he wants is hideous?"

"I know not to take the job."

"So in that sense," she persisted, not sure why she was being stubborn, but driven to it nonetheless, "you ensure that the client will approve what you like."

"Not ensure—" he dug in his own heels a little "—but I maximize the likelihood of it. And there's nothing wrong with that. It's the only sensible way to operate. Besides, the assumption is that the client comes to me because he likes my style."

"I don't know whether I like your style or not," she argued. "I haven't seen much of it."

She seemed to be taking a page from the past and deliberately picking a fight. As he'd done then, so now Carter fought back. "If you'd asked the other day, I'd have shown you pictures. I've got a portfolio full of them. You might have saved us both a whole lot of time and effort. But you were in such an all-fired rush to get back to your precious ivory tower—"

He caught himself only after he realized what he was doing. Jessica remained silent. He waited for her to rail at him the way she used to, but she didn't speak. In a far quieter voice he asked, "Are you still there?"

"Yes," she murmured, "but I don't know why. This isn't going to work. We're like fire and water."

"The past is getting in the way. Old habits die hard. But I'm sorry. What I said was unnecessary."

"Part of it was right," she conceded. "I was in a rush to get back. I had another appointment." He should know that he wasn't the only one in demand. "But as far as my ivory tower is concerned, that ivory tower has produced official interpreters for assorted summit meetings as well as for embassies in Moscow, Leningrad and Bonn. My work isn't all mind-in-the-clouds."

"I know," Carter said quietly. "I'm sorry." He didn't say anything more for a minute, hoping she'd tell him he was forgiven. But things weren't going to be so easy. "Anyway, I'd really like to talk again. Tell me when you have free time. If I have a conflict, I'll try to change it."

Short of being bitchy, which he'd accused her of being as a child, she couldn't turn her back on his willingness to accommodate her. She looked at the calendar tacked on the wall. It was filled with scrawled notations, more densely drawn for the upcoming few weeks. Given the choice, she would put off a meeting with Carter until after exams, when she'd be better able to take the disturbance in stride. But she remembered what he'd said about the weather. If she was going to do something with Crosslyn Rise, she wanted it done soon. The longer she diddled around with preliminary arrangements, the later in the season it would be and the greater the chance of winter closing in to delay the work even more. Instinctively she knew that the longer the process was drawn out, the more painful it would be.

"I'm free until noon next Tuesday morning," she said. "Do you want to come out and walk through Crosslyn Rise then?"

Carter felt a glimmer of excitement at the mention of walking through Crosslyn Rise. It had been years since he'd seen the place, and though he'd never lived there, since his parents had always rented a small house in town, returning to Crosslyn Rise would be something of a homecoming.

He had one meeting scheduled for that morning, but it was easily postponed. "Next Tuesday is fine. Time?"

"Is nine too early?"

"Nine is perfect. It might be a help if between now and then you wrote down your ideas so we can discuss them in as much detail as possible. If you've seen any pictures of things you like in newspapers or magazines you might cut them out. The more I know of what you want, the easier my job will be."

Efficient person that she was herself, she could go along with that. "You mentioned wanting to see a plot plan. I don't think I've ever seen one. Where would I get it?"

"The town should have one, but I'll take care of that. I can phone ahead and pick it up on my way. You just be there with your house and your thoughts." He paused. "Okay?"

"Okay."

"See you then."

"Uh-huh."

JESSICA COULDN'T DECIDE whether to put coffee on to brew or to assume that he'd already had a cup or two, and she spent an inordinate amount of time debating the issue. One minute she decided that the proper thing would indeed be to have it ready and offer him some; the next minute it seemed a foolish gesture. This was Carter Malloy, she told herself. He didn't expect anything from her but a hard time, which was just about all they'd ever given each other.

But that had been years ago, and Carter Malloy had changed. He'd grown up. He was an architect. A man. And though one part of her didn't want to go out of her way to make the Carter Malloy of any age feel welcome in her home, another part felt that she owed cordiality to the architect who might well play a part in her future.

As for the man in him, she pushed all awareness of that to the farthest reaches of consciousness and chose to attribute the unsettled feeling in her stomach to the nature of the meeting itself.

Carter arrived at nine on the dot. He parked his car on the pebbled driveway that circled some twenty feet in front of the ivy-draped portico. The car was dark blue and low, but Jessica wouldn't have known the make even if she'd had the presence of mind to wonder—which she didn't, since she was too busy trying to calm her nerves.

She greeted him at the front door, bracing an unsteady hand on the doorknob. Pulse racing, she watched him step inside, watched him look slowly around the rotundalike foyer, watched him raise his eyes to the top of the broadly sweeping staircase, then say in a low and surprisingly humble voice, "This is . . . very . . . weird."

"Weird?"

"Coming in the front door. Seeing this after so many years. It's incredibly impressive."

"Until you look closely."

He shot her a questioning glance.

"Things are worn," she explained, wanting to say it before he did. "The grandeur of Crosslyn Rise has faded."

"Oh, but it hasn't." He moved toward the center of the foyer. "The grandeur is in its structure. Nothing can dim that. Maybe the accessories have suffered with age, but the place is still a wonder."

"Is that your professional assessment?"

He shook his head. "Personal." His gaze was drawn toward the living room. The entrance to it was broad, the room itself huge. Knee-to-ceiling windows brought in generous helpings of daylight, saving the room from the darkness that might otherwise have come with the heavy velvet decor. Sun was streaming obliquely past the oversized fireplace, casting the intricate carving of the pine mantel in bas-relief. "Personal assessment. I always loved this place."

"I'm sure," she remarked with unplanned tartness.

He shot her a sharper look this time. "Does it gall you seeing me here? Does it prick your Victorian sensibilities? Would you rather I stay out back near the gardener's shed?"

Jessica felt instant remorse. "Of course not. I'm sorry. I was just remembering—"

"Remembering the past is a mistake, because what you remember will be the way I acted, not the way I felt. You didn't know the way I really felt. *I* didn't know the way I really felt a lot of the time. But I knew I loved this place."

"And you hated me because I lived here and you didn't."

"That's neither here nor there. But I did love Crosslyn Rise, and I'd like to feel free to express what I'm thinking and feeling as we walk around. Can I do that, or would you rather I repress it all?"

"You?" she shot back, goaded on by the fact that he was being so reasonable. "Repress your feelings?"

"I can do it if I try. Granted, I'm not as good at it as you. But you've had years of practice. You're the expert. No doubt there's a Ph.D. in Denial mixed up with all the diplomas on your wall." His eyes narrowed, seeing far too much. "Don't you ever get tired of bottling everything up?"

Jessica's insides were beginning to shake. She wanted to think it was anger, but that was only half-true. Carter was coming close to repeating things he'd said once before. The same hurt she'd felt then was threatening to engulf her now. "I don't bottle everything up," she said, and gave a tight swallow.

"You do. You're as repressed as ever." The words were no sooner out than he regretted them. She looked fearful, and for a horrifying minute, he wondered if she was going to cry. "Don't," he whispered and approached her with his hands out to the side. "Please. I'm sorry. Damn, I'm apologizing again. I can't believe that. Why do you make me say mean things? What is it about you that brings out the bastard in me?"

Struggling against tears, she didn't speak. A small shrug was the best she could muster.

"Yell at me," Carter ordered, willing to do anything to keep those tears at bay. "Go ahead. Tell me what you think of me. Tell me that I'm a bastard and that I don't know what I'm talking about because I don't know you at all. Say it, Jessica. Tell me to keep my mouth shut. Tell me to mind my own business. Tell me to go to hell."

But she couldn't do that. Deep down inside, she knew she was the villain of the piece. She'd provoked him far more than he'd provoked her. And he was right. She was repressed. It just hurt to hear him say it. Hurt a lot. Hurt even more, at thirty-three, than it had at sixteen.

Moving to the base of the stairs, she pressed herself against the swirling newel post, keeping her back to him. "I've lived at Crosslyn Rise all my life," she began in a tremulous voice. "For as long as I can remember, it's been my haven. It's the place I come home to, the place that's quiet and peaceful, the place that accepts me as I am and doesn't make demands. I can't afford to keep it up, so I have to sell it." Her voice fell to a tormented whisper. "That hurts, Carter. It really hurts. And seeing you—" she ran out of one breath, took in another "—seeing you brings back memories. I guess I'm feeling a little raw."

The warmth Carter had experienced the last time he'd been with Jessica was back. It carried him over the short distance to where she stood, brought his hands to her shoulders and imbued his low, slow voice with something surprisingly caring. "I can understand what you're feeling about Crosslyn Rise, Jessica. Really, I can." With the smallest, most subtle of movements, his hands worked at the tightness in her shoulders. "I wish I could offer a miracle solution to keep the Rise intact, but if there was one, I'm sure either you or Gordon would have found it by now. I can promise you that I'll draw up spectacular plans for the complex you have in mind, but it doesn't matter how spectacular they are, they won't be the Crosslyn Rise you've known all your life. The thought of it hurts you now, and it'll get worse before it gets better." He kept kneading, lightly kneading, and he didn't mind it at all. Her blouse was silk and soft, her shoulders surprisingly supple beneath it. His fingers fought for and won successive bits of relaxation.

"But the hurt will only be aggravated if we keep sniping at each other," he went on to quietly make his point. "I've already said I was wrong when I was a kid. If I could turn back the clock and change things, I would." Without thinking, he gathered a stray wisp of hair from her shoulder and smoothed it toward the tortoiseshell clasp at her nape. "But I can't. I can only try to make the present better and the future better than that—and 'try' is the operative word. I'll make mistakes. I'm a spontaneous person—maybe 'impulsive' is the word—but you already know that." He turned her to face him, and at the sight of her openness, gentled his voice even more. "The point is that I can be reasoned with now. I couldn't be back then, but I can be now. So if I say something that bugs you, tell me. Let's get it out in the open and be done."

Jessica heard what he was saying, but only peripherally. Between the low vibrancy of his voice and the slow, hypnotic motion of his hands, she was being warmed all over. Not even the fact that she faced him now, that she couldn't deny his identity as she might have if her back was still to him, could put a chill to that warmth.

"I'd like this job, Jessica," he went on, his dark eyes barely moving from hers yet seeming to touch on each of her features. "I'd really like this job, but I think you ought to decide whether working with me will be too painful on top of everything else. If it will be," he finished, fascinated by the softness of her cheek beneath the sweeping pad of his thumb, "I'll bow out."

His thumb stopped at the corner of her mouth, and time seemed to stop right along with it. In a flash of awareness that hit them simultaneously came the realization that they were standing a breath apart, that Carter was holding her as he would a desirable woman and Jessica was looking up at him as she would a desirable man.

She couldn't move. Her blood seemed to be thrumming through her veins in mockery of the paralysis of her legs, but she couldn't drag herself away from Carter. He gave her comfort. He made her feel not quite so alone. And he made her aware that she was a woman.

That fact took Carter by surprise. He'd always regarded Jessica as an asexual being, but something had happened when he'd put his hands on her shoulders. No, something had happened even before that, when she'd been upset and he'd wanted to help ease her through it. He felt protective. He couldn't remember feeling that for a woman before, mainly because most of the women he'd known were strong, powerful types who didn't allow for upsets. But he rather liked being needed. Not that Jessica would admit to needing him, he knew. Still, it was something to consider.

But he'd consider it another time, because she looked frightened enough at that minute to bolt, and he didn't want her to. Slowly, almost reluctantly, he dropped his hands to his sides.

A second later, Jessica dropped her chin to her chest. She raised a shaky hand to the bridge of her nose, pressed a fingertip to the nosepiece of her glasses and held it there. "I'm sorry," she whispered, sure that she'd misinterpreted what she'd seen and felt, "I don't know what came over me. I'm usually in better control of myself."

"You have a right to be upset," he said just as quietly, but he didn't step away. "It's okay to lose control once in a while."

She didn't look up. Nor did she say anything for a minute, because there was a clean, male scent in the air that held her captive. Then, cursing herself for a fool, she cleared her throat. "I, uh, I made coffee. Do you want some?"

What Carter wanted first was a little breathing space. He needed to distance himself mentally from the vulnerable Jessica, for whom he'd just felt a glimmer of desire. "Maybe we ought to walk around outside first," he suggested. "That way I'll know what you're talking about when you go through your list. You made one, didn't you?"

She met his gaze briefly. "Yes."

"Good." He remembered the feel of silk beneath his fingers. She was wearing a skirt that hit at midcalf; opaque stockings and flat shoes that would keep her warm, but her silk blouse, as gently as it fell over her breasts, wouldn't protect her from the air. "Do you want a sweater or something? It's still cool outside."

She nodded and took a blazer from the closet, quickly slipping her arms into the sleeves. Carter would have helped her with it if she hadn't been so fast. He wondered whether she wanted breathing space, too—then he chided himself for the whimsy. If Jessica had been struck in that instant with an awareness of him as a man, it was an aberration. No way was she going to allow herself to lust after Carter Malloy—*if* she knew the meaning of the word *lust*, which he doubted she did. And he certainly wasn't lusting after her. It was just that with his acceptance that she was a woman, she became a character of greater depth in his mind, someone he might like to get to know better.

They left through the front door, went down the brick walk and crossed the pebbled driveway to the broad lawn, which leveled off for a while before slanting gracefully toward the sea. "This is the best time of year," he remarked, taking in a deep breath. "Everything is new and fresh in spring. In another week or two, the trees will have budded." He glanced at Jessica, who was looking forlornly toward the shore, and though he doubted his question would be welcome, he couldn't pass by her sadness. "What will you do—if you decide to go ahead and develop Crosslyn Rise?"

It was a minute before she answered. Her hands were tucked into the pockets of her blazer, but her head was up and her shoulders straight. The fresh air and the walking were helping her to recover the equilibrium she'd lost earlier when Carter had been so close. "I'm not sure."

"Will you stay here?"

"I don't know. That might be hard. Or it might be harder to leave. I just don't know. I haven't gotten that far yet." She came to a halt.

Carter did, too. He followed her gaze down the slope of the lawn. "Tell me what you see."

"Something small and pretty. A marina. Some shops. Do you see how the boulders go? They form a crescent. I can see boats over there—" she pointed toward the far right curve of the crescent "—with a small beach and shops along the straightaway."

Carter wasn't sure he'd arrange the elements quite as she had, but that was a small matter. He started walking again. "And this slope?"

She came along. "I'd leave it as is, maybe add a few paths to protect the grass and some shrubbery here and there."

They descended the slope that led to the shoreline. "You used to sled down this hill. Do you remember?"

"Uh-huh. I had a Flexible Flyer," she recalled.

"New and shiny. It was always new and shiny."

"Because it wasn't used much. It was no fun sledding alone."

"I'd have shared that Flexible Flyer with you."

"Shared?" she asked too innocently.

"Uh, maybe not." He paused. "Mmm, probably not. I'd probably have chased you into the woods, buried you under a pile of snow and kept the Flyer all to myself."

Wearing a small, slightly crooked smile, she looked up at him. "I think so."

He liked the smile, small though it was, and it hadn't cracked her face after all. Rather, it made her look younger. It made him feel younger. "I was a bully."

"Uh-huh."

"You must have written scathing things about me in your diary."

"I never kept a diary."

"No? Funny, I'd have pegged you for the diary type."

"Studious?"

"Literary."

"I wrote poems."

He squinted as the memory returned. "That's . . . right. You did write poems."

"Not about you, though," she added quickly. "I wrote poems about pretty things, and there was absolutely nothing pretty about you that I could see back then."

"Is there now?" he asked, because he couldn't help it.

Jessica didn't know whether it was the outdoors, the gentle breeze stirring her hair or the rhythmic roll of the surf that lulled her, but her nervousness seemed on hold. She was feeling more comfortable than she had before with Carter, which was why she dared answer his question.

"You have nice skin. The acne's gone."

Carter was oddly pleased by the compliment. "I finally outgrew that at twenty-five. I had a prolonged adolescence, in *lots* of ways."

The subject of why he'd been such a troubled kid was wide open, but Jessica felt safer keeping things light. "Where did you get the tan?"

"Anguilla. I was there for a week at the beginning of March."

They'd reached the beach and were slowly crossing the rocky sand. "Was it nice?"

"Very nice. Sunny and warm. Quiet. Restful."

She wondered whether he'd gone alone. "You've never married, have you?"

"No."

On impulse, and with a touch of the old sarcasm, she said, "I'd have thought you'd have been married three times by now."

He didn't deny it. "I probably would have, if I'd let myself marry at all. Either I knew what a bad risk I was, or the women I dated did. I'd have made a lousy husband."

"Then. What about now?"

Without quite answering the question, he said, "Now it's harder to meet good women. They're all very complex by the time they reach thirty, and somehow the idea of marrying a twenty-two-year-old when I'm nearly forty doesn't appeal to me. The young ones aren't mature enough, the older ones are too mature."

"Too mature—as in complex?"

He nodded and paused, slid his hands into the pockets of his dark slacks and stood looking out over the water. "They have careers. They have established life-styles. They're stuck in their ways and very picky about who they want and what they expect from that person. It puts a lot of pressure on a relationship."

"Aren't you picky?" she asked, feeling the need to defend members of her sex, though she'd talked to enough single friends to know that Carter was right.

"Sure I'm picky," he said with a bob of one shoulder. "I'm not getting any younger. I have a career and an established life-style, and I'm pretty set in my ways, too. So I'm not married." He looked around, feeling an urge to change the subject. "Were you thinking of keeping the oceanfront area restricted to people who live here?"

"I don't know. I haven't thought that out yet." She studied the crease on his brow. "Is there a problem?"

"Problem? Not if you're flexible about what you want. As I see it, either you have a simple waterfront with a beach and a pier and a boat house or you have a marina with a dock, slips, shops and the appropriate personnel to go with them. But if you want the marina and the shops, they can't be restricted—at least, not limited to the people who live here. You could establish a private yacht club that would be joined by people from all along the North Shore, and you can keep it as exclusive as you want by regulating the cost of membership, but there's no way something as restrictive as that is going to be able to support shops, as I think of shops." As he talked, he'd been looking around, assessing the beachfront layout. Now he faced her. "What kind of shops did you have in mind?"

"The kind that would provide for the basic needs of the residents—drugstore, convenience store, bookstore, gift or crafts shop." She saw him shaking his head. "No?"

"Not unless there's public access. Shops like that couldn't survive with such a limited clientele base."

Which went to show, Jessica realized in chagrin, how little she knew about business. "But I was thinking really *small* shops. Quaint shops."

"Even the smallest, most quaint shop has to do a certain amount of business to survive. You'd need public access."

"You mean, scads of people driving through?" But that wasn't at all what she wanted, and the look on her face made that clear.

"They wouldn't have to drive through. The waterfront area could be arranged so that cars never cross it."

"I don't know," she murmured, disturbed. Turning, she headed back up toward the house.

He joined her, walking for a time in silence before saying, "You don't have to make an immediate decision."

"But you said yourself that time was of the essence."

"Only if you want to get started this year."

"I don't *want* to get started at all," she said, and quickened her step.

Knowing the hard time she was having, he let her go. He stayed several paces behind until she reached the top of the rise, where she slowed. When he came alongside her, she raised her eyes to his and asked in a tentative voice, "Were you able to get the plot plan?"

He nodded. "It's in the car."

"Do you want to take it when we go through the woods?"

"No. I'll study it later. What I want is for you to show
me the kinds of settings you had in mind for the housing.
Even though ecological factors will come into play when
a final decision is made, your ideas can be a starting point."
He took a deep breath, hooked his hands on his hips and
made a visual sweep of the front line of trees. "I used to go
through these woods a lot, but that was too many years
ago and never with an eye out for something like this."

She studied his expression, but it told her nothing of
what he was feeling just then, and she wanted to know.
She was feeling frighteningly upended and in need of support. "You said that you really wanted this project." She
started off toward a well-worn path, confident that Carter would fall into step, which he did.

"I do."

"Why?"

"Because it's an exciting one. Crosslyn Rise is part of my
past. It's a beautiful place, the challenge will be to maintain its beauty. If I can do that, it will be a feather in my
cap. So I'll have the professional benefit, and the personal
satisfaction. And if I invest in the project the way Gordon
proposed, I'll make some money. I could use the money."

That surprised her. "I thought you were doing well."

"I am. But there's a luxury that comes with having spare
change. I'd like to be able to reject a lucrative job that may
be unexciting and accept an exciting job that may not be
lucrative."

His argument was reasonable. *He* was reasonable—far
more so than she'd have expected. Gordon had said he'd
changed. *Carter* had said he'd changed. For the first time,
as they walked along the path side by side, with the dried
leaves of winter crackling beneath their shoes, she wondered what had caused the change. Simple aging? She
doubted it. There were too many disgruntled adults in the

world to buy that. It might have been true if Carter had simply mellowed. But given the wretch of a teenager he'd been, mellowing was far too benign a term to describe the change. She was thinking total personality overhaul—well, not total, since he still had the occasional impulsive, sharp-tongued moment, but close.

For a time, they walked on without talking. The crackle of the leaves became interspersed with small, vague sounds that consolidated into quacks when they approached the duck pond. Emerging from the path into the open, Jessica stopped. The surface of the pond and its shores were dotted with iridescent blue, green and purple heads. The ducks were in their glory, waiting for spring to burst forth.

"There would have to be some houses here, assuming care was taken to protect the ducks. It's too special a setting to waste."

Carter agreed. "You mentioned cluster housing the other day. Do you mean houses that are physically separate from one another but clustered by twos and threes here and in other spots? Or clusters of town houses that are physically connected to one another?"

"I'm not sure." She didn't look at him. It was easier that way, she found. The bobbing heads of the ducks on the pond were a more serene sight. But her voice held the curiosity her eyes might have. "What do you think?"

"Off the top of my head, I like the town house idea. I can picture town houses clustered together in a variation on the Georgian theme."

"Wouldn't that be easier to do with single homes?"

"Easier, but not as interesting." He flashed her a self-mocking smile, which, unwittingly looking his way, she caught. "And not as challenging for me. But I'd recommend the town house concept for economic reasons, as well. Take this duck pond. If you build single homes into the setting, you wouldn't want to do more than two or three, and they'd have to be in the million-plus range. On the other hand, you could build three town house clusters, each with two or three town houses, and scatter them around. Since they could be marketed for five or five-fifty, they'd be easier to sell and you'd still come out ahead."

She remembered when Gordon had spoken of profit. Her response was the same now as it was then, a sick kind of feeling at the pit of her stomach. "Money isn't the major issue."

"Maybe not to you—"

"Is it to you?" she cut in, eyeing him sharply.

He held his ground. "It's one of the issues, not necessarily the major one. But I can guarantee you that it *will* be the major issue for the people Gordon lines up to become part of his consortium. You and I have personal feelings for Crosslyn Rise. The others won't. They may be captivated by the place and committed to preserving as much of the natural contour as possible, but they won't have an emotional attachment. They'll enter into this as a financial venture. That's all."

"Must you be so blunt?" she asked, annoyed because she knew he was right, yet the words stung.

"I thought you'd want the truth."

"You don't have to be so *blunt*." She turned abruptly and, ignoring the quacks that seemed stirred by the movement, headed back toward the path.

"You want sugarcoating?" He took off after her. "Where are you going now?"

"The meadow," she called over her shoulder.

With a minimum of effort, he was by her side. "Y'know, Jessica, if you're going ahead with this project, you ought

to face facts. Either you finance the whole thing yourself—"

"If I had that kind of money, there wouldn't *be* any
project!"

"Okay, so you don't have the money." He paused, irked
enough by the huffy manner in which she'd walked away
from him to be reckless. "Why don't you have the money?
I keep asking myself that. Where did it go? The Crosslyn
family is loaded."

"Was loaded."

"Where did it go?"

"How do *I* know where it went?" She whirled around
to face him. "I never needed it. It was something my father had that he was supposedly doing something brilliant with. I never asked about it. I never cared about it.
So what do I know?" She threw up a hand. "I've got my
head stuck in that ivory tower of mine. What do I know
about the money that's supposed to be there but isn't?"

He caught her hand before it quite returned to her side.
"I'm not blaming you. Take it easy."

"Take it easy?" she cried. "The single most stable thing
in my life is on the verge of being bulldozed—by *my* decision, no less—and you tell me to take it easy? Let go of
my hand."

But he didn't. His long fingers wound through hers.
"Changing Crosslyn Rise may be upsetting, but it's not the
end of the world. It's just a house, for heaven's sake."

"It's my family's history."

"So now it's time to write a new chapter. Crosslyn Rise
will always be Crosslyn Rise. It's not going away. It's just
getting a face-lift. Wouldn't you rather have it done now,
when you can be there to supervise, than have it done
when you die? It's not like you have a horde of children to
leave the place to."

Of all the things he'd said, that hurt the most. The issue of having a family, of passing something of the Crosslyn genes to another generation had always been a sensitive issue for Jessica. Her friends didn't raise it with her. Not even Gordon had made reference to it during their discussion of Crosslyn Rise. The fact that Carter Malloy was the one to twist the knife was too much to bear.

"Let me go," she murmured, lowering both her head and her voice as she struggled to free her hand from his.

"No."

She twisted her hand, even used her other one to try to pry his fingers free. Her teeth were clenched. "I want you to let me go."

"I won't. You're too upset."

"And you're not helping." She lifted her eyes then, uncaring that he saw the tears there. "Why do you have to say things that hurt so much?" she said softly. "Why do you do it, Carter? You could always find the one thing that would hurt me most, and that was the thing you'd harp on. You say you've changed, but you're still hurting me. Why? Why can't you just do your job and leave me alone?"

Seconds after she'd said it, Carter asked himself the same question. It should have been an easy matter to approach this job as he would another. But he was emotionally involved—as much with Jessica as with Crosslyn Rise—which was why, without pausing to analyze the details of that emotional involvement, he reached out, drew Jessica close and wrapped her in his arms.

4

WHEN CARTER HAD BEEN A KID, he'd imagined that Jessica Crosslyn was made of nails. He'd found a hint of give when he'd touched her earlier, but only when he held her fully against him, as he did now, did he realize that she was surprisingly soft. Just as surprising was the tenderness he felt. He guessed it had to do with the tears he'd seen in her eyes. She was fighting them still, he knew. He could feel it in her body.

Lowering his head so that his mouth wasn't far from her ear, he said in a voice only loud enough to surmount the whispering breeze, "Let it out, Jessica. It's all right. No one will think less of you, and you'll feel a whole lot better."

But she couldn't. She'd been too weak in front of Carter already. Crying would be the last straw. "I'm all right," she said, but she didn't pull away. It had been a long time since someone had held her. She wasn't yet ready to have it end, particularly since she was still in the grip of the empty feeling brought on by his words.

"I don't do it intentionally," he murmured in the same deeply male, low-to-the-ear voice. "Maybe I did when we were kids, but not now. I don't intentionally hurt you, but I blurt out things without thinking." Which totally avoided the issue of whether the things he blurted out were true, but that was for another time. For now there were more immediate explanations to be offered. "I'm sorry for that, Jessica. I'm sorry if I hurt you, and I know I ought to be able to do my job and leave you alone, but I can't. Maybe it's because I knew you back then, so there's a bond. Maybe it's because your parents are gone and you're alone. Maybe it's because I owe you for all I put you through."

"But you're putting me through more," came the meek voice from the area of his shirt collar.

"Unintentionally," he said. His hands flexed, lightly stroking her back. "I know you're going through a hard time, and I want to help. If I could loan you the money to keep Crosslyn Rise, I'd do it, but I don't have anywhere near enough. Gordon says you've got loans on top of loans."

"See?" The reminder was an unwelcome one. "You're doing it again."

"No, I'm explaining why I can't help out more. I've come a long way, but I'm not wealthy. I couldn't afford to own a place like Crosslyn Rise myself. I have a condo in the city, and it's in a luxury building, but it's small."

"I'm not asking—"

"I know that, but I want to do something. I want to help you through this, maybe make things easier. I guess what I'm saying is that I want us to be friends."

Friends? Carter Malloy, her childhood nemesis, a friend? It sounded bizarre. But then, the fact that she was leaning against him, taking comfort from his strength was no less bizarre. She hadn't imagined she'd ever want to touch him, much less feel the strength of his body. And he was strong, she realized—physically and, to her chagrin, emotionally. She could use some of that strength.

"I'm also thinking," he went on, "that I'd like to know more about you. When we were kids, I used to say awful things to you. I assumed you were too stuck-up to be bothered by them."

"I was bothered. They hurt."

"And if I'd known it then," he acknowledged honestly, "I'd probably have done it even more. But I don't want to do that now. So if I know what you're thinking, if I know what your sore spots are, I can avoid hitting them. Maybe I can even help them heal." He liked that idea. "Sounds lofty, but if you don't aim high, you don't get nowhere."

"Anywhere," she corrected, and raised her head. There was no sarcasm, only curiosity in her voice. "When did you become a philosopher?"

He looked down into her eyes, dove gray behind her glasses. "When I was in Vietnam. A good many of the things I am now I became then." At her startled look, he was bemused himself. "Didn't you guess? Didn't you wonder what it was that brought about the change?"

She gave a head shake so tiny it was almost imperceptible. "I was too busy trying to deny it."

"Deny it all you want, but it's true. I'll prove it to you if you let me, but I can't do it if you jump all over me every time I say something dumb." When she opened her mouth to argue, he put a finger to her lips. "I can learn, Jessica. Talk to me. Reason with me. Explain things to me. I'm not going to turn around and walk away. I'll listen."

Her fingers tightened on the crisp fabric of his shirt just above his belt, and her eyes went rounder behind her glasses. "And then what?" she asked, still without sarcasm. In place of her earlier curiosity, though, was fear. "Will you take what I've told you and turn it on me? If you wanted revenge, that would be one way to get it."

"Revenge?"

"You've always hated what I stood for."

He shook his head slowly, his eyes never once leaving hers. "I thought I hated it, but it was me I hated. That was one of the things I learned a while back. For lots of reasons, some of which became self-perpetuating, I was an unhappy kid. And I'm not saying that all changed over-night. I spent four years in the army. That gave me lots of time to think about lots of things. I was still thinking about them when I got back." His hands moved lightly just above her waist. "That last time when I saw you I was still pretty unsettled. You remember. You were sixteen."

The memory was a weight, bowing her head, and the next thing she knew she felt Carter's jaw against her crown, and he was saying very softly, "I treated you poorly then, too."

"That time was the worst. I was so unsure of myself anyway, and what you said—"

"Unsure of yourself?" His hands went still. "You weren't."

"I was."

"You didn't look it."

"I felt it. It was the second date I'd ever had." The words began to flow and wouldn't stop. "I didn't like the boy, and I didn't really want to go, but it was so important to me to be like my friends. They dated, so I wanted to date. We were going to a prom at his school, and I had to wear a formal dress. My mother had picked it out in the store, and it looked wonderful on her, but awful on me. I didn't have her face or her body or her coloring. But I put on the dress and the stockings and the matching shoes, and I let her do my hair and face. Then I stood on the front porch looking at my reflection in the window, trying to pull the dress higher and make it look better . . . and you came around the corner of the house. You told me that I could pull for-ever and it wouldn't do any good, because there was nothing there worth covering. You said—"

"Don't, Jessica—"

"You said that any man worth beans would be able to see that right off, but you told me that I probably didn't have anything to worry about, because you doubted any-one who would ask me out was worth beans. But that was no problem, either, you told me—"

"Please—"

"Because, you said, I was an uptight nobody, and the only thing I'd ever have to offer a man would be money. I could buy someone, you said. Money was power, you said, and then—"

"Jessica, don't—"

"And then you reached into your pocket, pulled out a dollar bill and stuffed it into my dress, and you said that I should try bribing my date and maybe he'd kiss me."

She went quiet, slightly appalled that she'd spilled the whole thing and more than a little humiliated even seventeen years after the fact. But she couldn't have taken back the words if she'd wanted to, and she didn't have time to consider the damage she'd done before Carter took her face in his hands and turned it up.

"Did he kiss you?"

She shook her head as much as his hold would allow.

"Then I owe you for that, too," he whispered, and before she could begin to imagine what he had in mind, his mouth touched hers. She tired to pull back, but he held her, brushing his mouth back and forth over her lips until their stiffness eased, then taking them in a light kiss.

It didn't last long, but it left her stunned. Her breath came in shallow gasps, and for a minute she couldn't think. That was the minute when she might have identified what she felt as pleasure, but when her heart began to thud again and her mind started to clear, she felt only disbelief. "Why did you do that?" she whispered, and lowered her eyes when disbelief gave way to embarrassment.

"I don't know." He certainly hadn't planned it. "I guess I wanted to. It felt right."

"You shouldn't have," she said, and exerted pressure to lever herself away. He let her go. Immediately she felt the loss of his body heat and drew her blazer closer around her. Mustering shreds of dignity, she pushed her glasses up on her nose and raised her eyes to his. "I think we'd better get going. There's a lot to cover."

She didn't wait for an answer, but moved off, walking steadily along the path that circled the rear of the house. She kept her head high and her shoulders straight, looking far more confident than she felt. Instinct told her that it was critical to pretend the kiss hadn't happened. She couldn't give it credence, couldn't let on she thought twice about it, or Carter would have a field day. She could just imagine the smug look on his face even now, which was why she didn't turn. She knew he was following, could hear the crunch of dried leaves under his shoes. No doubt he was thinking about what a lousy kisser she was.

Because he sure wasn't. He was an incredible kisser, if those few seconds were any indication of his skill. Not that she'd liked it. She couldn't possibly *like* Carter Malloy's kiss. But she'd been vulnerable at that moment. Her mind had been muddled. She was definitely going to have to get it together unless she wanted to make an utter fool of herself.

How to get it together, though, was a problem. She was walking through land that she loved and that, a year from then, wouldn't be hers, and she was being followed by a demon from her past who had materialized in the here and now as a gorgeous hunk of man. She had to think business, she decided. For all intents and purposes, in her dealings with Carter she was a businesswoman. That was all.

They walked silently on until the path opened into a clearing. Though the grass was just beginning to green up after the winter's freeze, the lushness of the spot as it would be in full spring or high summer was lost on neither of them. They had the memories to fill in where reality lay half-dormant.

Jessica stopped at the meadow's mouth. When Carter reached her side, she said, "Another grouping of homes should go here. It's so pretty, and it's already open. That means fewer trees destroyed. I want to disturb as little of the natural environment as possible."

"I understand," Carter said, and walked on past her into the meadow. He was glad he understood something. He sure didn't understand why he'd kissed her—or why he'd found it strangely sweet. Unable to analyze it just then, though, he strode along one side of the four-acre oval, stopping several times along the way to look around him from a particular spot. After standing for a time in deep concentration at the far end, he crossed back through the center.

And all the while, with nothing else to do and no excuse not to, Jessica studied him. Gorgeous hunk of man? Oh, yes. His clothes—heathery blazer, slate-colored slacks, crisp white shirt—were of fine quality and fitted to perfection, but the clothes didn't make him a gorgeous hunk. What made him that was the body beneath. He was broad shouldered, lean of hip and long limbed, but even then he wouldn't have been as spectacular if those features hadn't all worked together. His body flowed. His stride was smooth and confident, the proud set of his head perfectly comfortable on those broad shoulders, his expression male in a dark and mysterious way.

If he felt her scrutiny, it obviously didn't affect him at all. But then, she mused, he was probably used to the scrutiny of women. He was the type to turn heads.

With a sigh, she turned and started slowly back on the path. It was several minutes before Carter caught up with her. "What do you think?" she asked without looking at him.

"It would work."

"If you'd like more time there, feel free. You can meet me up at the house."

"Are you cold?" he asked, because she was still hugging the blazer around her.

"No. I'm fine."

He glanced back toward the meadow, "Well, so am I. This is just a preliminary walk-through. I've seen enough for now. What's next?"

"The pine grove."

That surprised him. "Over on the other side of the house?" When she nodded, he said, "Are you sure you want to build there?"

She looked up at him then. "I need a third spot. If you can think of someplace better, I'm open for suggestion."

Drudging up what he remembered of the south end of the property, he had to admit that the pine grove seemed the obvious choice. "But that will mean cutting. The entire area is populated with trees. There isn't any sizable clearing to speak of, not like at the duck pond or in the meadow." He shook his head. "I'd hate to have to take down a single one of those pines."

Jessica took in a deep breath and said sadly, "So now you know what I'm feeling about this project. It's a travesty, isn't it? But I have no choice." Determined to remain strong and in control, she turned her eyes forward and continued on.

For the first time, Carter did know what she felt. It was one thing when he was dealing with the idea—and his memory—of Crosslyn Rise, another when he was walking there, seeing, smelling and feeling the place, being surrounded by the natural majesty that was suddenly at the mercy of humans.

When they reached the pine grove, he was more acutely aware of that natural majesty than ever. Trees that had been growing for scores of years stretched toward the heavens as though they had an intimate connection with the place. Lower to the ground were younger versions, even lower than that shrubs that thrived in the shade. The carpeting underfoot was a tapestry of fine moss and pine needles. The pervasive scent was distinct and divine.

I have no choice, Jessica had said on a variation of the theme she'd repeated more than once, and he believed her. That made him all the more determined to design something special.

Jessica was almost sorry when they returned to the house. Yes, she was a little chilled, though she wouldn't have said a word to Carter lest, heaven forbid, he offer her his jacket, but the wide open spaces made his masculinity a little less commanding. Once indoors, there would be nothing to dilute it.

"You'll want to go through the house," she guessed, more nervous as they made their way across the back porch and entered the kitchen.

"I ought to," he said. "But that coffee smells good. Mind if I take a cup with me?"

She was grateful for something to do. "Cream or sugar?"

"Both."

As efficiently as possible, given the awkwardness stirring inside her, she poured him a mugful of the dark brew and prepared it as he liked it.

"You aren't having any?" he asked when she handed him the mug.

She didn't dare. Her hands were none too steady, and caffeine wouldn't help. "Maybe later," she said, and in as businesslike a manner as she could manage, led him off on a tour of the house.

The tour should have been fairly routine through the first floor, most of which Carter had seen at one time or another. But he'd never seen it before with a knowledge of architecture, and that made all the difference. High ceilings, chair rails and door moldings, antique mantelpieces on the three other first-floor fireplaces—he was duly impressed, and his comments to that extent came freely.

His observations were professional enough to lessen the discomfort Jessica felt when they climbed the grand stairway to the second floor. Still she felt discomfort aplenty, and she couldn't blame it on the past. Something had happened when Carter had kissed her. He'd awoken her to the man he was. Her awareness of him now wasn't of the boy she'd hated but of the man she wished she could. Because that man was calm, confident and commanding, all the things she wanted to be just then, but wasn't. In comparison to him, she felt inadequate, and, feeling inadequate, she did what she could to blend into the woodwork.

It worked just fine as they made their way from one end of the long hall down and around a bend to the other end. Carter saw the once-glorious master bedroom that hadn't been used in years; he saw a handful of other bedrooms, some with fireplaces, and more bathrooms than he'd ever dreamed his mother had cleaned. He took everything in, sipping his coffee as he silently made notes in his mind. Only when he reached the last bedroom, the one by the back stairs, did his interest turn personal.

"This is yours," he said. He didn't have to catch her nod to know that it was, but not even the uncomfortable look on her face could have kept him from stepping inside. The room was smaller than most of the others and decorated more simply, with floral wallpaper and white furniture.

Helpless to stop himself, he scanned the paired bookshelves to find foreign volumes and literary works fully integrated with works of popular fiction. He ran a finger along the dresser, passed a mirrored tray bearing a collection of antique perfume bottles and paused at a single framed photograph. It was a portrait of Jessica with her parents when she was no more than five years old; she looked exactly as he remembered her. It was a minute before he moved on to an old trunk, painted white and covered with journals, and an easy chair upholstered in the same faded pastel pattern as the walls. Then his gaze came to rest on the bed. It was a double bed, dressed in a nubby white spread with an array of lacy white pillows of various shapes and sizes lying beneath the scrolled headboard.

The room was very much like her, Carter mused. It was clean and pure, a little welcoming, a little off-putting, a little curious. It was the kind of room that hinted at exciting things in the nooks and crannies, just beyond the pristine front.

Quietly, for quiet was what the room called for, he asked, "Was this where you grew up?"

"No," she said quickly, eager to answer and return downstairs. "I moved here to save heating the rest of the house."

The rationale was sound. "This is above the kitchen, so it stays warm."

"Yes." She took a step backward in a none-too-subtle hint, but he didn't budge. In any other area of the house, she'd have gone anyway and left him to follow. But this was her room. She couldn't leave him alone here; that would have been too much a violation of her private space.

"I like the picture," he said, tossing his head toward the dresser. A small smile played at the corner of his mouth. "It brings back memories."

She focused on the photograph so that she wouldn't have to see his smile. "It's supposed to. That was a rare family occasion."

"What occasion?"

"Thanksgiving."

He didn't understand. "What's so rare about Thanksgiving?"

"My father joined us for dinner."

Carter studied her face, trying to decide if she was being facetious. He didn't think so. "You mean, he didn't usually do it?"

"It was hit or miss. If he was in the middle of something intense, he wouldn't take a break."

"Not even for Thanksgiving dinner?"

"No," she said evenly, and met his gaze. "Are you done here? Can we go down?"

He showed no sign of having heard her. "That's really incredible. I always pictured holidays at Crosslyn Rise as being spectacular—you know, steeped in tradition, everything warm and pretty and lavish."

"It was all that. But it was also lonely."

"Was that why you married so young?" When her eyes flew to his, he added, "My mother said you were twenty."

She wanted to know whether he'd specifically asked for the details and felt a glimmer of annoyance that he might be prying behind her back. Somehow, though, she couldn't get herself to be sharp with him. She was tired of sounding like a harpy when his interest seemed so innocent.

"Maybe I was lonely. I'm not sure. At the time I thought I was in love."

Obviously she'd changed her mind at some point, he mused. "How long did it last?"

"Didn't your mother tell you that?"

"She said it was none of my business, and it's not. If you don't want to talk about it, you don't have to.

Jessica rested against the doorjamb. She touched the wood, rubbed a bruised spot. "It's no great secret." It was, after all, a matter of public record. "We were divorced two years after we married."

"What happened?"

She frowned at the paint. "We were different people with different goals."

"Who was he?"

She paused. "Tom Chandler." Her arm stole around her middle. "You wouldn't have known him."

"Not from around here?"

She shook her head. "Saint Louis. I was a sophomore in college, he was a senior. He wanted to be a writer and figured that I'd support him. He thought we were rich." The irony of it was so strong that she was beyond embarrassment. Looking Carter in the eye, she said, "You were right. Bribery was about the only way I'd get a man. But it took me two years to realize that was what had done it."

Carter came forward, drawn by the pallor of her face and the haunted look in her eyes, either of which was preferable to the unemotional way she was telling him something that had to be horribly painful for her. "I don't understand."

"Tom fell in love with Crosslyn Rise. He liked the idea of living on an estate. He liked the idea of my father being a genius. He liked the idea of my mother devoting herself to taking care of my father, because Tom figured that was what I'd do for him. Mostly, he liked the idea of turning the attic into a garret and spending his days there reading and thinking and staring out into space."

"Then you tired of the marriage before he did?"

"I . . . suppose you could say that. He tired of me pretty quickly, but he was perfectly satisfied with the marriage. That was when I realized my mistake."

There was a world of hurt that she wasn't expressing, but Carter saw it in her eyes. It was all he could do not to reach out to help, but he wasn't sure his help would be welcome. So he said simply, "I'm sorry."

"Nothing to be sorry about." She forced a brittle smile. "Two years. That was all. I was finishing my undergraduate degree, so I went right on for my Ph.D., which was what I'd been planning to do all along."

"I'm sorry it didn't work out. Maybe if you'd had someone to help with the situation here—"

"Not Tom. Forget Tom. He was about as adept with finances as my mother and twice as disinterested."

"Still, it might not have been so difficult if you hadn't been alone."

She tore her eyes from his. "Yes, well, life is never perfect." She looked at the bright side, which was what she'd tried hard to do over the years. "I have a lot to be grateful for. I have my work. I love that, and I do it well. I've made good friends. And I have Crosslyn—" she caught herself and finished in a near whisper "—Crosslyn Rise." Uncaring whether he stayed in her room or not, she turned and went quickly down the back stairs.

When Carter joined her, Jessica was standing stiffly at the counter, taking a sip of the coffee she'd poured herself. Setting the mug down, she raised her chin and asked, "So, where do we go from here as far as this project is concerned?"

Carter would have liked to talk more about the legacy of her marriage, if only to exorcise that haunted look from her eyes. His good sense told him, though, that such a discussion was better saved for another time. He was surprised that she'd confided in him as much as she had. Friends did that. It was a good sign.

"Now you talk to me some more about what you want," he said. "But first I have to get my briefcase from the car. I'll be right back."

Left alone in the kitchen for those few short moments, Jessica took several long, deep breaths. She didn't seem able to do that when Carter was around. He was a physical presence, dominating whatever room he was in. But she couldn't say that the domination was deliberate—or offensive, for that matter. He was doing his best to be agreeable. It wasn't his fault that he was so tall, or that his voice had such resonance, or that he exuded an aura of power.

"Do you have the list?" he asked, striding back into the kitchen. When she nodded and pointed to a pad of paper waiting on the round oak table nearby, he set his briefcase beside it. Then he retrieved his coffee mug. "Mind if I take a refill?"

"Of course not." She reached for the glass carafe and proceeded to fix his coffee with cream and sugar, just as he'd had it before. When he protested that he could do it, she waved him away. She was grateful to be active and efficient.

Carrying both mugs, she led him to the table, which filled a semicircular alcove off the kitchen. The walls of the alcove were windowed, offering a view of the woods that had enchanted Jessica on many a morning. On this morning, she was too aware of Carter to pay much heed to the pair of cardinals decorating the Douglas fir with twin spots of red.

"Want to start from the top?" Carter asked, eyeing her list.

She did that. Point by point, she ran through her ideas. Most were ones she'd touched on before, but there were others, smaller thoughts—ranging from facilities at the clubhouse to paint colors—that had come to her and seemed worth mentioning. She began tentatively and gained courage as she went.

Carter listened closely. He asked questions and made notes. Though he pointed out the downside of some of her ideas, not once did he make her feel as though something she said was foolish. Often he illustrated one point or another by giving examples from his own experience, and she was fascinated by those. Clearly he enjoyed his work and knew what he was talking about. By the time he rose to leave, she was feeling surprisingly comfortable with the idea of Carter designing the new Crosslyn Rise.

That comfort was from the professional standpoint.

From a personal standpoint, she was feeling no comfort at all. For no sooner had that low blue car of his purred down the driveway than she thought about his kiss. Her pulse tripped, her cheeks went pink, her lips tingled—all well after the fact. On the one hand, she was gratified that she'd had such control over herself while Carter had been there. On the other hand, she was appalled at the extent of her reaction now that he was gone.

Particularly since she hadn't liked his kiss.

But she had. She had. It had been warm, smooth, wet. And it had been short. Maybe that was why she'd liked it. It hadn't lasted long enough for her to be nervous or frightened or embarrassed. Nor had it lasted long enough to provide much more than a tempting sample of something new and different. She'd never been given a kiss like that before—not from a date, of which there hadn't been many of the kissing type, and certainly not from Tom. Tom had been as self-centered in lovemaking as he'd been in everything else. A kiss from Tom had been a boring experience.

Carter's kiss, short though it was, hadn't been boring at all. In fact, Jessica realized, she wouldn't mind experiencing it again—which was a *truly* dismaying thought. She'd never been the physical type, and to find herself entertaining physical thoughts about Carter Malloy was too much.

Chalking those thoughts up to a momentary mental quirk, she gathered her things together and headed for Cambridge.

The diversionary tactic worked. Not once while she was at work did she think of Carter, and it wasn't simply that she kept busy. She took time out late in the afternoon for a relaxed sandwich break with two male colleagues, then did some errands in the Square and even stopped at the supermarket on her way home—none of which were intellectually demanding activities. Her mind might have easily wandered, but it didn't.

No, she didn't think about Carter until she got home, and then, as though to make up for the hours before, she couldn't escape him. Every room in the house held a memory of his presence, some more so than others. Most intensely haunted were the kitchen and her bedroom, the two rooms in which she spent the majority of her at-home hours. Standing at the bedroom door as she had done when he'd been inside, sitting once again at the kitchen table, she saw him as he'd been, remembered every word he'd said, felt his presence as though he were there still.

It was the recency of his visit, she told herself, but the rationalization did nothing to dismiss the memories. By walking through her home, by looking at all the little things that were intimate to her, he had touched her private self.

She wanted to be angry. She tried and tried to muster it, but something was missing. There was no offense. She didn't feel violated, simply touched.

And that gave her even more to consider. The Carter she'd known as a kid had been a violater from the start; the Carter who had reentered her life wasn't like that at all. When the old Carter had come near, she'd trembled in anger, indignation and, finally, humiliation; when the new Carter came near, the trembling was from something else.

She didn't want to think about it, but there seemed no escape. No sooner would she immerse herself in a diversion than the diversionary shell cracked. Such was the case when she launched into her nightly workout in front of the VCR; rather than concentrate on the routine or the aerobic benefits of the exercise, she found herself thinking about body tone and wondering whether she looked better at thirty-three for the exercise she did, than she'd looked at twenty-five. And when she wondered why she cared, she thought of Carter.

When, sweaty and tired, she sank into a hot bath, she found her body tingling long after she should have felt pleasantly drowsy, and when she stopped to analyze those tingles, she thought of Carter.

When, wearing a long white nightgown with ruffles at the bodice, she settled into the bedroom easy chair, with a lapful of reading matter that should have captured her attention, her attention wandered to those things that Carter had seen and touched. She pictured him as he had stood that morning, looking tall and dark, uncompromisingly male, and curious about her. She spent a long time thinking about that curiosity, trying to focus in on its cause.

She was without conclusions when the phone rang by her bed. Startled, she picked it up after the first ring, but the sudden stretch sent the books on her lap sliding down the silky fabric of her gown to the floor. She made a feeble attempt to catch them at the same time that she offered a slightly breathless, "Hello?"

Carter heard that breathlessness and for an awful minute wondered if he'd woken her. A glance at his watch told him it was after ten. He hadn't realized it was so late. "Jessica? This is Carter." He paused. "Am I catching you at a bad time?"

Letting the books go where they would, she put a hand to her chest to still her thudding heart. "No. No. This is fine."

"I didn't wake you?"

"No. I was reading." Or trying to, she mused, but her mind didn't wander farther. It was waiting for Carter's next words. She couldn't imagine why he'd called, particularly at ten o'clock at night.

Carter wasn't sure, either. Nothing he had to say couldn't wait for another day or two, certainly for a more reasonable hour. But he'd been thinking about Jessica for most of the day. They had parted on good terms. He wanted to know whether those good terms still stood, or whether she'd been chastising herself for this, that and the other all day. And beyond that, he wanted to hear her voice.

Relieved now that he hadn't woken her, he leaned back against the strip of kitchen wall where the phone hung. "Did you get to school okay today?"

"Uh-huh."

"Everything go all right? I mean, I didn't get you going off on the wrong foot or anything, did I?"

She gave a shy smile that he couldn't possibly see, but it came though in her voice. "No. I was fine. How about you?"

"Great. It was a really good day. I think you bring me good luck."

She didn't believe that for a minute, but her smile lingered. "What happened?"

Carter was still trying to figure it out. "Nothing momentous. I spent the afternoon in the office working on other projects, and a whole bunch of little things clicked. It was one of those days when I felt really in tune with my work."

"Inspired?"

"Yeah." He paused, worried that she'd think he was simply trying to impress her. "Does that sound pretentious?"

"Of course not. It sounds very nice. We should all have days like that."

"Yours wasn't?"

She thought back on what she'd done since she'd seen him that morning. "It was," she said, but cautiously. "It's an odd time. I gave the final lecture to my German lit class, and I was really pleased with the way it went, but the meetings I had after that were frustrating."

Carter was just getting past the point of picturing her with her nose stuck in a book all day. He wanted to know more about what she did. "In what way?"

"At the end of the term, students get nervous. They're realizing that a good part of their grade is going to depend on a final exam, a term paper or both. If they go into these last two weeks with a solid average, they're worried about keeping it up. If they go in with a low average, they're desperate to raise it. Even the most laid-back of them get a little uptight."

"Didn't you when you were in school?"

"Sure. So I try to be understanding. It's mostly a question of listening to them and giving them encouragement. That's easy to do if I know the student. I can concentrate on his strengths and relate the class material to it. If I don't know the student, it's harder, sort of like stabbing in the dark at the right button to help the student make the connection."

Carter was quiet for a minute. Then he said, "I'm impressed. You're a dedicated professor, to put that kind of thought into interactions with students. The professors I studied under weren't like that. They were guarded, almost like they saw us as future competition, so they wanted us to learn, but not too much."

She knew some colleagues who were like that, and though she couldn't condone the behavior, she tried to explain it by saying, "You were older when you started college."

"Not that much. I was twenty-three."

"But you were wise in a worldly way that was probably intimidating."

A day or a week before, Carter might have taken the observation as an offense. That he didn't take it that way now was a comment on how far he'd come in terms of self-confidence where Jessica was concerned. It was also an indication of how far she'd come; her tone was gentle, conversational, which was how he kept his. "How did you know I was world wise at twenty-three?" She'd seen so little of him then.

"You were that way at seventeen, and you were very definitely intimidating."

He thought back to those years with an odd blend of nostalgia and self-reproach. "I tried to be. Lord, I tried. Intimidating people was about the only thing I was good at."

"You could have been good at other things. Look where you are now. That talent didn't suddenly come into being when you hit your twenties. But you let everyone think you had no brains."

"I thought it, too. I was messed up in so many other ways that no brains seemed part of the package."

Jessica wanted to ask him about being messed up. She wanted to know the why and how of it. She wanted to be able to make some sense of the person he'd been and relate it to the person he was now. Because this person was interesting. She could warm to this Carter as she would never have dreamed of doing to the one who had once been malicious.

The irony of it was that in some ways the new Carter was more dangerous.

"Are you still there?" he asked.

"Uh-huh," she answered as lightly as she could given the irregular skip of her pulse.

He figured he was either making her uncomfortable by talking about the past or boring her, and he didn't want to do either, not tonight, not when they finally seemed to be getting along. So he cleared his throat. "You're probably wondering why I called."

She was, now that he mentioned it. A man like Carter Malloy wouldn't call her just to talk. "I figured you'd get around to it in good time," she said lightly. She wanted him to know that she was taking the call in stride, just as she'd taken his kiss in stride. It wouldn't do for him to know that she was vulnerable where he was concerned.

"Well, now's the time. When I was driving back to town from Crosslyn Rise this morning, it occurred to me that it might help both of us if you were to see some of the other things I've done."

"I saw those sketches—"

"Not sketches. The real thing. I've done other projects similar in concept to the one you want done. If you were to see them in person, you might get a feeling for whether I'm the right man for this job."

Jessica felt something heavy settle around her middle. "You're having second thoughts about working here."

"It's not—"

"You can be honest," she said, tipping up her chin. "I'm not desperate. There are plenty of other architects."

"Jessica—"

"The only reason Gordon suggested you was because you were familiar with the Rise. He figured you'd be interested."

"I *am*," Carter said loudly. "Will you please be quiet and let me speak?" When he didn't hear anything coming from the other end of the line, he breathed, "Thank you. My Lord, Jessica, when you get going, you're like a steamroller."

"I don't want to play games. That's all. If you don't want this job, I'd appreciate your coming right out and saying so, rather than beating around the bush."

"I *want* this job. I *want* this job. How many times do I have to say it?"

More quietly she said, "If you want it, why were you looking to give me an out?"

"Because I want you to *choose* me," he blurted. Standing well away from the wall now, he ran his fingers through his hair. "I'd like to feel," he said slowly, "that you honestly want me to do the work. That you're *enthusi-*

astic about my doing it. That it isn't just a case of Gordon foisting me on you, or your not having the time or energy to interview others."

She was thinking that he wasn't such a good businessman after all. "You're an awful salesman. You should be tooting your own horn, not warning me off. Are you this way with all your clients?"

"No. This case is different. You're special."

His words worked wonders on the heaviness inside her. She felt instantly lighter, and it didn't matter that he'd meant the words in the most superficial of ways. What he'd said made her feel good.

"Okay," she breathed. "I'm sorry I interrupted."

Stunned by the speed and grace of her capitulation, Carter drew a blank. For the life of him, he couldn't remember what had prompted the set-to. "Uh . . ."

"You were saying that maybe I ought to see some of the things you've done."

Gratefully he picked up the thread. "The best ones—the ones I like best—are north of you, up along the coast of Maine. The farthest is three hours away. They could all be seen in a single day." He hesitated for a second. "I was thinking that if you'd like, we could drive up together."

It was Jessica's turn to be stunned. The last thing she'd expected was that Carter would want to spend a day with her, even on business. Her words come slowly and skeptically. "Isn't that above and beyond the call of duty?"

"What do you mean?"

"You don't have to go to such extremes. I can drive north myself."

"Why should you have to go alone if I'm willing to take you?"

"Because that would be a whole day out of your time."

"So what else is my time for?"

"Working."

"I get plenty of work done during the week. So do you, and you said you were coming up on exams. I was thinking of taking a Sunday when both of us can relax."

That was even *more* incredible. "I can't ask you to take a whole Sunday to chauffeur me around!"

"Why not?"

"Because Sundays are personal, and this would be business."

"It could be fun, too. There are some good restaurants. We could stop and get something to eat along the way."

Jessica returned her hand to her chest in an attempt to slow the rapid beat of her heart.

"Or you could shop," he went on. "There are some terrific boutique areas. I wouldn't mind waiting."

She was utterly confused. "I couldn't ask you to do that."

"You don't have to ask. I'm offering." He was struck by an afterthought that hardened his voice. "Unless you'd rather not be with me for that length of time."

"That's not it."

"Then what is?"

"*Me.* Wouldn't you rather not be with *me* for that length of time? You'll be bored to tears. I'm not the most dynamic person in the world."

"Who told you that?"

"You. When I was ten, you caught me sitting on the rocks, looking out to sea. You asked what I saw, and when I wouldn't answer, you said I was dull and pathetic."

He felt like a heel. "You were only ten, and I was full of it."

"But Tom agreed. He thought I was boring, too. I've never been known as the life of the party."

"Sweetheart, a man can only take being with the life of the party for so long. Let me tell you, *that* can get boring. You, on the other hand, have a hell of a lot going for you." He let the flow of his thoughts carry him quickly on. "You read, you think, you work. Okay, so you don't open up easily. That doesn't mean you're boring. All it means is that a man has to work a little harder to find out what's going on in that pretty head of yours. I'm willing to work a little harder. I think the reward will be worth it. So you'd be doing me a favor by agreeing to spend a Sunday with me driving up the coast." He took a quick breath, not allowing himself the time to think about all he'd said. "What'll it be—yes or no?"

"Yes," Jessica said just as quickly and for the very same reason.

5

JESSICA HAD A DREAM that night. It brought her awake gradually, almost reluctantly, to a dark room and a clock that read 2:24 a.m. Her skin was warm and slightly damp. Her breath was coming in short whispers. The faint quivering deep inside her was almost a memory, but not quite.

She stretched. When the quivering lingered, she curled into a ball to cradle it, because there was something very nice about the feeling. It was satisfying, soft and feminine.

Slowly, even more slowly than she'd awoken, she homed in on the subject of her dream. Her reluctance this time had nothing to do with preserving a precious feeling. As Carter Malloy's image grew clearer in her mind, the languorous smile slipped from her face. In its place came a look of dismay.

Jessica had never had an erotic dream before. Never. Not when she'd been a teenager first becoming aware of her developing body, not when she'd been dating Tom, not in the long years following the divorce. She wasn't blind to a good-looking man; she could look at male beauty, recognize it, admire it for what it was. But it had never excited her in a physical sense. It had never buried itself in her subconscious and come forward to bring her intense pleasure in the middle of the night.

Flipping to her other side, she shielded her face with her arm, as if to hide her embarrassment from a horde of grinning voyeurs masked by the dark.

Carter Malloy. Carter Malloy, beautifully naked and splendidly built. Carter Malloy, coming to her, kissing her, stroking her. He'd been exquisitely gentle, removing her clothes piece by piece, loving her with his hands and his mouth, driving her to a fever pitch that she'd never experienced before.

With a moan, she flipped back to the other side and huddled under the covers, but the sheet that half covered her face couldn't blot out the persistent images in her mind. Carter Malloy, kissing her everywhere, *everywhere*, while he offered his own body for her eager hands and lips. In her dream, he was large and leanly muscled, textured at some spots, smooth and vulnerable at others, very, very hard and needy at still others.

Sitting bolt upright in bed, she turned on the lamp, hugged her knees to her chest and worked to ground herself among the trappings of the old and familiar. To some extent she was successful. At least the quivering inside her eased. What she was left with, though, was an undertone of frustration that was nearly as unwelcome.

She couldn't understand it. She just wasn't a passionate person. Lovemaking with Tom had been a part of marriage that she'd simply accepted. Occasionally she'd enjoyed it. Occasionally she'd even had an orgasm, though she could count the number of times that had happened on the fingers of one hand. And she hadn't minded that it was so infrequent. Sex was a highly overrated activity, she had long since decided.

That didn't explain why she'd dreamed what she did, or why the dream had brought her to a sweet, silent climax.

Mortified anew, she pressed her eyes to her knees. What if someone had seen her? What if someone had been watching her sleep? Not that anyone would have or could have seen her, still she wondered if she had made noise, or writhed about.

It was something she'd eaten, she decided. Certain foods were known to stir up the senses. Surely that was what had brought on the erotic interlude.

But she went over every morsel of food that had entered her mouth that day—easy to do, since she was neither a big eater nor an adventurous one—and she couldn't single out anything that might have inspired eroticism.

Maybe, she mused, it had to do with her own body. Maybe she was experiencing a hormonal shift, maybe even related to menopause. But she was only thirty-three! She wasn't ready for menopause!

The hormonal theory, though, had another twist. They said that women reached their peak of sexual interest at a later age than men. Women in their thirties and forties were supposed to be hot—at least, that was what the magazines said, though she'd always before wondered whether the magazines said it simply because it was what their thirty- and forty-year-old readers wanted to hear.

Maybe there was some truth to it, though. Maybe she was developing needs she'd never had before. She had been a long time without a man, better than eleven years. Maybe the dream she'd had was her body's way of saying that it was in need. Maybe that need even had to do with the biological clock. Maybe her body was telling her that it was time to have a baby.

Throwing the covers back, she scrambled from the bed, grabbed her glasses and, barefoot, half walked, half ran down the back steps to the kitchen. Soon after, she was sitting cross-legged on one of the chairs with an open tin of Poppycock nestled in her lap.

Poppycock was her panacea. When she'd been little, she had hidden it in her room, because her mother had been convinced that the caramel coating on the popcorn would rot her teeth. Now that her mother wasn't around to worry, Jessica kept the can within easy reach. It wasn't that she pigged out on a regular basis, and since she didn't have a weight problem, it probably wouldn't have mattered if she had, but Poppycock was a treat. It was light and fun, just the thing she went for when she was feeling a little down.

She wasn't feeling down now, but frustrated and confused. She was also feeling angry, angry at Carter, because no matter how long she made her list of possible excuses for what had happened, she knew it wasn't coincidence that had set Carter Malloy's face and body at the center of her dream. She cursed him for being handsome and sexy, cursed herself for being vulnerable, cursed Crosslyn Rise for aging and putting her into a precarious position.

One piece of popcorn followed another into her mouth. In time, she helped herself to a glass of milk, and by the time that was gone, it was well after three. Having set her mind to thinking about the material she had to cover in her Russian seminar that afternoon, she'd calmed down some. With a deep, steady breath, she rose from the chair, put the empty glass into the sink and the tin of Poppycock into the pantry, and went back to bed.

WHEN JESSICA HAD AGREED to drive north with Carter, he had wanted to do it that Sunday for the sake of getting her feedback as soon as possible. She had put him off for a week, knowing that she had far too much work to do in preparation for exams, to take off for the whole day. In point of fact, the following Sunday wouldn't be much better; though she had teaching assistants to grade exams, she always did her share, and she liked it that way.

But Carter was eager, and she knew that she could plan around the time. So they had settled on the day, and he had promised to call her the Saturday before to tell her when he would be picking her up. She wasn't scheduled to hear from him until then, and in the aftermath of that embarrassingly carnal dream, she was grateful for the break. Given twelve days' time, she figured she could put her relationship with him into its proper perspective.

That perspective, she decided had to be business, which was what she thought about during those days when she had the free time to let her mind wander. She concentrated on the business of converting Crosslyn Rise into something practical and productive—and acclimating herself to that conversion.

To that end, she called Nina Stone and arranged to meet her for dinner at a local seafood restaurant, a chic establishment overlooking the water on the Crosslyn Rise end of town. The two had met the year before, browsing in a local bookstore, and several months after that, Jessica had approached her about selling Crosslyn Rise. Though Nina hadn't grown up locally, she'd been working on the North Shore for five years, and during that time she had established herself as an aggressive broker with both smarts and style. She was exactly the kind of woman Jessica had always found intimidating, but strangely, they'd hit it off. Jessica could see Nina's tough side, but there was a gentler, more approachable side as well. That side came out when they were together and Nina let down her defenses.

Despite her reputation, despite the aggressiveness Jessica knew was there, Nina had never pressured her. She was like Carter in the sense that, having come from nothing, she was slightly in awe of Crosslyn Rise—which meant that she was in no rush to destroy it.

For that reason among others, Jessica felt comfortable sharing the latest on the Rise with her.

"A condominium community?" Nina asked warily. She was a small woman, slender and pixieish, which made her assertiveness in business somewhat unexpected and therefore all the more effective. "I don't know, Jessica. It would be a shame to do that to such a beautiful place."

"Condominium communities can be beautiful."

"But Crosslyn Rise is that much more so."

Jessica sighed. "I can't afford it, Nina. You've known that for a while. I can't afford to keep it as it is, and you haven't had any luck finding a buyer."

"The market stinks," Nina said, sounding defensive, looking apologetic. "I'm selling plenty on the low and middle end of the scale, but precious little at the top." She grew more thoughtful. "Condos are going, though, I do have to admit. Particularly in this area. There's something about the ocean. Young professionals find it romantic, older ones find it restful." She paused to sip her wine. Her fingers were slender, her nails polished red to match her suit. "Tell me more. If this was Gordon Hale's idea, I would guess that it's financially sound. The man is a rock. You say he's putting together a consortium?"

"Not yet, but he will when it's time. Right now, I'm working with someone to define exactly what it is that I want."

"Someone?"

After the slightest hesitation, she specified, "An architect."

Nina studied her for a minute. "You look uncomfortable."

Jessica pushed her glasses up on her nose. "No."

"Is this architect a toughie?"

"No. He's very nice. His name is Carter Malloy." She watched for a reaction. "Ever heard of him?"

"Sure," Nina said without blinking an eye. "He's with Malloy and Goodwin. He's good."

Jessica felt a distant pride. "You're familiar with his work, then?"

"I saw something he did in Portsmouth not long ago. Portsmouth isn't my favorite place, but this was beautiful. He had converted a textile mill into condos. Did an incredible job combining old and new." She frowned, then grinned at the same time. "If I recall correctly, the man himself is beautiful."

"I don't know as I'd call him beautiful," Jessica answered, but a little too fast, and that roused Nina's interest.

"What would you call him?"

She thought for a minute. "Pleasant looking."

"Not the man I remember. Pleasant looking is someone you'd pass by and smile at kindly. A beautiful man stirs stronger emotions. Carter Malloy was ruggedly masculine—at least, in the picture I saw."

"He is masculine looking, I suppose."

Nina came forward, voice lowered but emphatically chiding. "You suppose, my foot! I can't believe you're as immune to men as you let on. One lousy husband can't have neutered you, and you're not exactly over the hill. You have years of good fun still ahead, if you want to make something of them." She raised her chin. "Who was the last man you dated?"

Jessica shrugged.

"Who?" Nina prodded, but good-naturedly as she settled back in her seat. "You must remember."

"It's a difficult question. How do you define a date? If it's going somewhere with a man, I do that all the time with colleagues."

"That's not what I mean, and you know it. I'm talking about the kind of date who picks you up at your house, takes you out for the evening, kisses you when he brings you home, maybe even stays the night."

"Uh, I'm not into that."

"Sleeping with men?"

"Are you?" Jessica shot back, in part because she was uncomfortable doing the answering and in part because she wanted to know. She and Nina had become friends in the past year, but the only thing Jessica knew about her social life was that she rarely spent a Saturday night at home.

Nina was more amused than anything. "I'm not into sleeping around, but I do enjoy men. There are some nice ones around who are good for an evening's entertainment. Since I'm not looking to get married, I don't threaten them."

"You don't want to get married?"

"Honey, do I have the time?"

"Sure. If you want."

"What I want," Nina said, sitting back in her chair, looking determined but vulnerable, "is to make good money for myself. I want my own business."

"I thought you were making good money now."

"Not enough."

"Are you in need?"

"I've been in need since the day I learned that my mother prostituted herself to put milk on our table."

Jessica caught in a breath. "I'm sorry, Nina. I didn't know."

"It's not something I put on the multiple-listings chart," she quipped, but her voice was low and sober. "That was in Omaha. I have a fine life for myself here, but I won't ever sell myself like my mother did. So I need money of my own. I refuse to ever ask a man for a cent, and I won't have to, if I play my cards right."

"You're doing so well."

"I could be doing even better if I went out on my own. But I'll have to hustle."

Jessica was getting a glimpse of the driven Nina, the one who was restless, whose mind was always working, whose heart was prepared to sacrifice satisfaction for the sake of security. Jessica found it sad. "But you're only thirty."

"And next year I'll be thirty-one, and thirty-two the year after that. The way I figure it, if I work my tail off now and go independent within a year, by the time I'm thirty-five, I can be the leading broker in the area, with a fully trained staff, to boot. Maybe then I'll be able to ease up a little, even think of settling down." She gave a crooked smile. "Assuming there are any worthwhile men out there then."

"If there are, you'll find them," Jessica said, and felt a shaft of the same kind of envy she'd known as a child, when all the other girls were prettier and more socially adept than she. Nina had short, shiny hair, flawless skin and delicate bones. She dressed on the cutting edge between funky and sophisticated and had a personality to match. "You draw people like honey draws bees."

"Lucky for me, or I'd be a loss at what I do." She paused to give Jessica a look that was more cautious than clever. "So I've made the ultimate confession. And you? Do you ever think of settling down?"

Jessica smiled and shook her head. "I don't attract men the way you do."

"Why not?" Nina asked, perfectly serious. "You're smart and pretty and gainfully employed. Aren't those the things men look for nowadays?

Pretty. Carter had used that word. *A man has to work a little harder to find out what's going on in that pretty head of yours.* It was an expression, of course, not to be taken seriously. "Men look for eye-catching women like you."

"And once they've done the eye-catching, they take a closer look and see the flaws. No man would want me right now. I'm too hard. But you're softer. You're established. You're confident in ways I'm not."

"What ways?" Jessica shot back in disbelief.

"Financial. You have Crosslyn Rise."

"Not for long," came the sad reminder.

While the waiter served their lobsters, Nina considered that. As soon as he left, she began to speak again. "You're still a wealthy woman, Jessica. The problem is fluidity of funds. You don't have enough to support the Rise because your assets are tied up *in* the Rise. If you go through with the project you've mentioned, you'll emerge with a comfortable nest egg. Besides, you don't have the fear—" she paused to tie the lobster bib around her neck "—of being broke that I have. You're financially sound, and you're independent. That gives you a head start in the peace-of-mind department. So all you have to do—" she tore a bright red feeler from the steaming lobster "—is to find a terrific guy, settle down somewhere within commuting distance of Harvard and have babies."

"I don't know," Jessica murmured. She was looking at her lobster as though she weren't sure which part to tackle first. "Things are never that simple."

"You watch. Things will get easier when this business with the Rise is settled." That said, she began to suck on the feeler.

Jessica, too, paused to eat, but she kept thinking about Nina's statement. After several minutes, she asked, "Are we talking about the same 'things'?"

"Men. We're talking about men."

"But what does my settling the Rise have to do with men?"

"You'll be freer. More open to the idea of a relationship." When Jessica's expression said she still didn't make the connection, Nina said, "In some respects, you've been wedded to the Rise. No—" she held up a hand "—don't take this the wrong way. I'm not being critical. But in the time I've known you, I've formed certain impressions. Crosslyn Rise is your haven. You've lived there all your life. Even when you married, you lived there."

"Tom wanted it."

"I'm sure he did. Still, you lived there, and when the marriage fell apart, he left and you were alone there again."

"I wasn't alone. My parents were there."

"But you're alone now, and you're still there. Crosslyn Rise is like a companion."

"It's a house," Jessica protested.

But Nina had a point to make. "A house with a presence of its own. When you're there, do you feel alone?"

"No."

"But you should—not that I'm wishing loneliness on you, but man wasn't put on earth to live in solitude."

"I'm with people all day. I like being alone at night."

"Do you?" she asked, arching a delicately shaped brow. "I don't. But then, my place isn't steeped in the kind of memories that Crosslyn Rise is. If I were to come home and be enveloped by a world of memories, I probably wouldn't feel alone, either." She stopped talking, poked at the lobster with her fork for a distracted minute, then looked up at Jessica. "Once Crosslyn Rise is no longer yours in the way that it's always been, you may need something more."

Jessica shot her a despairing look. "Nothing like the encouragement of a friend."

"But it *is* encouragement. The change will be good for you. More so than any other person I know, you've had a sameness to your life. Coming out from the shadow of Crosslyn Rise will be exciting."

The image of the shadow stuck in Jessica's mind. The more she mulled it over, the more she realized that it wasn't totally bizarre. "Do you think I hide behind the Rise?" It was a timid question, offered to a friend with the demand for an honest answer.

Nina gave it as she saw it. "To some extent. Where your work is concerned, you've been as outgoing as anyone else. Where your personal life is concerned, you've fallen back on the Rise, just because it's always been there. But you can stand on your own in any context, Jessica. If you don't know that now, you will soon enough."

SOON ENOUGH WASN'T AS SOON as Jessica wanted. At least, that was what she was thinking the following Sunday morning as she dressed to spend the day driving north with Carter. He'd called her the morning before to ask if eight was too early to come. It wasn't; she was an early riser. Her mind was freshest during those first postdawn hours. She did some of her most productive work then.

She didn't feel particularly productive on Sunday morning, though. Nor, after mixing, matching and discarding four different outfits did she feel particularly fresh. She couldn't decide what to wear, because the occasion was strange. She and Carter certainly weren't going on a date. This was business. Still, he'd mentioned stopping for something to eat, maybe even shopping, and those weren't strictly business ventures. A business suit was too formal, jeans too casual, and she didn't want to wear a teaching ensemble, because she was *tired* of wearing teaching ensembles.

At length, she decided on a pair of gabardine slacks and a sweater she'd bought in the Square that winter. The sweater was the height of style, the saleswoman had told her, but Jessica had bought it because it was slouchy and comfortable. For the first time, she was glad it was stylish, too. She was also glad it was a pale gray tweed, not so much because it went with her eyes but because it went with the slacks, which, being black, were more sophisticated than some of her other things.

For a time, she distracted herself wondering why she wanted to look sophisticated. She should look like herself, she decided, which was more down-to-earth than sophisticated. But that didn't stop her from matching the outfit up with shiny black flats, from dusting the creases of her eyelids with mocha shadow, from brushing her hair until it shone and then coiling it into a neat twist at the nape of her neck.

She was a bundle of nerves by the time Carter arrived, and the situation wasn't helped by his appearance. He looked wonderful—newly showered and shaved, dressed in a burgundy sweater and light gray corduroy pants.

Taking her heavy jacket from her, he stowed it in the trunk of the car with his own. He held the door while she slipped into the passenger's seat, then circled the car and slid behind the wheel.

"I should warn you," Jessica said when he started the car, "that I'm a terrible passenger. If you have any intention of speeding, you'll have a basket case on your hands."

"Me? Speed?"

Without looking at him, she sensed his grin. "I can remember a certain squealing of tires."

"Years and years ago, and if it'll put your mind at ease,
the last accident I had was when I was nineteen," Carter
answered with good humor, and promptly stepped on the
gas. He didn't step on it far, only enough to maintain the
speed limit once they'd reached the highway, and not once
did he feel he was holding back. Sure, there were times
when he was alone in the car and got carried away by the
power of the engine, but he wasn't a reckless driver. He
certainly didn't vent his anger on the road as he used to do.

But then, he didn't feel the kind of anger at the world
that he used to feel. He rarely felt anger at all—frustration, perhaps, when a project that he wanted didn't come
through, or when one that did wasn't going right, or when
one of the people under him messed up, or when a client
was being difficult—but not anger. And he wasn't feeling
any of those things at the moment. He'd been looking forward to this day. He was feeling lighthearted and re-
freshed, almost as though the whole world was open to
him just then.

He took his eyes from the road long enough to glance at
Jessica. Her image was already imprinted on his mind, put
there the instant she'd opened her front door, but he
wanted a moment of renewed pleasure.

She looked incredibly good, he thought, and it wasn't
simply a matter of having improved with age. He'd noted
that improvement on the two other occasions when he'd
seen her, but seeing her today took it one step further. She
was really pretty—adorable, he wanted to say, because the
small, round glasses sitting on her nose had that effect on
her straight features, but her outfit was a little too serious
to be called adorable. He liked the outfit. It was subtle but

UP TO 6 FREE GIFTS FOR YOU!
Look inside—all gifts are absolutely free!

If offer card is missing write to:
Harlequin Reader Service, 3010 Walden Ave., P.O. Box 1867, Buffalo, NY 14269-1867

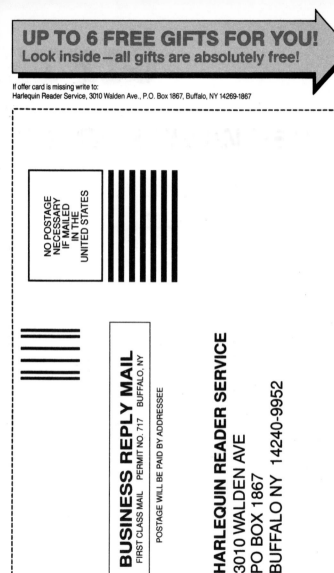

NO POSTAGE
NECESSARY
IF MAILED
IN THE
UNITED STATES

BUSINESS REPLY MAIL
FIRST CLASS MAIL   PERMIT NO. 717   BUFFALO, NY

POSTAGE WILL BE PAID BY ADDRESSEE

HARLEQUIN READER SERVICE
3010 WALDEN AVE
PO BOX 1867
BUFFALO NY 14240-9952

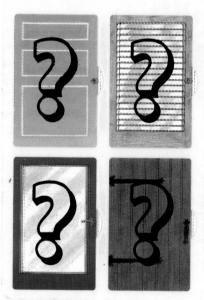

stylish, and seemed perfectly suited to who she was. He was pleased to have her in the car with him. She added the class that he never quite believed he'd acquired.

"Comfortable?" he asked.

She darted him a quick glance. "Uh-huh."

He let that go for several minutes, then asked, "How are exams going?"

"Pretty well," she said on an up note.

"You sound surprised."

"I never know what to expect. There have been years when it's been one administrative foul-up after another—exams aren't printed on time, or they're delivered to the wrong place, that kind of thing."

"At Harvard?" he teased.

She took his teasing with a lopsided smile. "At Harvard. This year, the Crimson has done itself proud."

"I'm glad of that for your sake."

"So am I," she said with a light laugh, then sobered. "Of course, now the rush begins to get things graded and recorded. Graduation isn't far off. The paperwork has to be completed well before then."

"Do you go to graduation?"

"Uh-huh."

"Must be. . . uplifting."

Her laugh was more of a chuckle this time, and a facetious one at that. Carter took pleasure in the sound. It said that she didn't take herself or her position too seriously, which was something he needed to know, given all the years he'd assumed she was stuck-up. She didn't seem that way, now. More, she didn't seem conscious of any social difference between them. He was convinced that the more he was with her, architect to client, the less she'd think back on the past, and that was what he wanted.

He wanted even more, though. Try as he might, he couldn't forget the time he'd kissed her. It had been an impulsive moment, but it had stuck in his mind, popping up to taunt him when he least expected it.

Jessica was, he decided during one of those times, the rosebud that hadn't quite bloomed. Having been married, she'd certainly been touched, but Carter would put money on the fact that her husband hadn't lit any fires in her. Her mouth was virginal. So was her body, the way she held it, not frightened so much as unsure, almost naive.

Carter had never been a despoiler of virgins. Even in his wildest days, he'd preferred women who knew the score. Tears over blood-stained sheets or unwanted pregnancies or imagined promises weren't his style. So he'd gone with an increasingly savvy woman—exactly the kind who now left him cold.

Kissing Jessica, albeit briefly, hadn't left him cold. He'd felt warm all over, then later, when he'd had time to remember the details of that kiss, tight all over. It amazed him still, it really did. That Jessica Crosslyn, snotty little prude that she'd been, should turn him on was mind-boggling.

But she did turn him on. Even now, with his attention on driving and the gearshift and a console between them, he was deeply aware of her—of the demure way she crossed her legs and the way that caused her slacks to outline shapely thighs, of the neat way her hands lay in her lap, fingers slender and feminine, of the loose way her sweater fell, leaving an alarmingly seductive hint of her breasts beneath. Even her hair, knotted with such polish, seemed a parody of restraint. So many things about her spoke of a promise beneath the facade. And she seemed totally unaware of it.

Maybe it was his imagination. Maybe the sexy things he was seeing were simply things that had changed in her, and it was his lecherous mind that was defining them as sexy. He saw women often, but it had been a while since he'd slept with one. Maybe he was just horny.

If that was true, of course, he could have remedied the situation through tried and true outlets. But he wasn't interested in those outlets. He wasn't running for any outlet at all. There was a sweetness to the arousal Jessica caused; there was something different and special about the tightness in his groin. He wasn't exactly sure where it would take him, but he wasn't willing it away just yet.

"You got a vote of confidence from a friend of mine," Jessica told him as they safely sped north. "She said she'd seen a project you did in Portsmouth."

"Harborside? I was thinking we'd hit that last, on the way home."

"She was impressed with it."

He shrugged. "It's okay, but it's not my favorite."

"What is?"

"Cadillac Cove. I hate the name, but the complex is special."

"Who decides on the name?"

"The developer. I just do the designs."

Jessica had been wondering about that. "Just the designs? Is your job done when the blueprints are complete?"

"Sometimes yes, sometimes no. It depends on the client. Some pay for the blueprints and do everything else on their own. Others pay me to serve as an advisor, in which case I'm involved during the actual building. I like it that way—" he speared her with a cautioning look "—and it has nothing to do with money. Moneywise, my time's better spent working at a drafting table. But there's satisfaction in being at the site. There's satisfaction seeing a concept take form. And there's peace of mind knowing that I'm available if something goes wrong."

"Do things go wrong often? I've heard some nightmarish stories. Are they true?"

"Sometimes." He curved his long fingers more comfortably around the wheel. "Y'see, there's a basic problem with architectural degrees. They fail to require internships in construction. Most architects and would-be architects see themselves as a step above. They're the brains behind the construction job, so they think, but they're wrong. They may be the inspiration, and the brains behind the overall plan, but the workmen themselves, the guys with the hammers and nails, are the ones with the know-how. The average architect doesn't have any idea how to build a house. So, sometimes the average architect draws things into a blueprint that can't possibly be built. Forget things that don't look good. I'm talking about sheer physical impossibilities."

A bell was ringing in Jessica's mind. "Didn't Gordon say you had hands-on building experience?"

"I spent my summers during college working on construction."

"You knew all along you wanted to be an architect?"

"No." He smirked. "I knew I needed money to live on, and construction jobs paid well." The smirk faded. "But that was how I first became interested in architecture. Blueprints intrigued me. The overall designs intrigued me. The guys who stood there in their spiffy suits, wearing hardhats, intrigued me." He chuckled. "So did the luxury cars they drove. And they all drive them. Porsches, Mercedes sportsters, BMWs—this Supra is modest compared to my colleagues' cars."

"So why don't you have a Porsche?"

"I was asking myself that same question the other day when my partner showed me his new one."

"What's the answer?"

"Money. They're damned expensive."

"You're doing as well as your partner."

He shrugged. "Maybe I don't trust myself not to scratch it up. Or it could be stolen. I don't have a secured garage space. I park in a narrow alley behind my building." He pursed his lips and thought for a minute before finally saying in a quieter voice, "I think I'm afraid that if I buy a Porsche, I'll believe that I've made it, and that's not true. I still have a ways to go."

Jessica was reminded of Nina, who defined happiness as a healthy bank account. Instinctively she knew that wasn't the case with Carter. He wasn't talking about making it economically, but professionally.

Maybe even personally. But that was a guess. She didn't know anything of his hopes and dreams.

On that thought, she lapsed into silence. Though she was curious, she didn't have the courage to suddenly start asking him about hopes and dreams, so she gave herself up to the smooth motion of the car and the blur of the passing landscape. The silence was comfortable, and surprising in that Jessica had always associated silence with solitude. Usually when she was with a man in a nonacademic setting, she felt impelled to talk, and since she wasn't the best conversationalist in the world, she wound up feeling awkward and inadequate.

She didn't feel that way now. The miles that passed beneath the wheels of the car seemed purpose enough. Moreover, if Carter wanted to talk, she knew he would. He wasn't the shy type—which was really funny, the more she thought of it. She'd always gravitated toward the shy type, because with the shy type she felt less shy herself. But in some ways it was easier being with Carter, because at any given time she knew where she stood.

At that moment in time, she knew that he was as comfortable with the silence as she was. His large hands were relaxed on the wheel, his legs sprawled as much as the car would allow. His jaw—square, she noted, like his chin—was set easily, as were his shoulders. He made no effort to speak, other than to point out something about a sign or a building they passed that had a story behind it, but when the tale was told, he was content to grow quiet again.

They drove straight for nearly four hours—with Carter's occasional apology for the lengthy drive, and a single rest stop—to arrive shortly before noon at Bar Harbor.

The drive was worth it. "I'm impressed," Jessica said sincerely when Carter had finished showing her around Cadillac Cove. Contrary to Crosslyn Rise, the housing was all oceanfront condominiums, grouped in comfortable clusters that simultaneously managed to hug the shore and echo the grace of nearby Cadillac Mountain. "Is it fully sold?"

He nodded. "Not all of the units are occupied year-round. This far north, they wouldn't necessarily be. A lot of them are owned on a time-sharing plan, and I think one or two are up for resale, but it's been a profitable venture for the developer."

"And for you."

"I was paid for my services as an architect, and I've cashed in on the praise that the complex has received, but I didn't have a financial stake in the project the way I might with Crosslyn Rise."

"Has Gordon talked with you more about that?"

"No. How about you?"

She shook her head. "I think he's starting to put feelers out, but he doesn't want to line up investors until we give him something concrete to work with."

Carter liked the "we" sound. "Does he work with a list of regular investors?"

"I don't really know." Something on his face made her say, "Why?"

"Because I know of a fellow who may be interested. His name's Gideon Lowe. I worked with him two years ago on a project in the Berkshires, and we've kept in touch. He's an honest guy, one of the best builders around, and whether or not he serves as the contractor for Crosslyn Rise, he may want to invest in it. He's been looking for something sound. Crosslyn Rise is sound."

"So you say."

"So I *know*. Hey, I wouldn't be investing my own money in it if it weren't." Without skipping a beat, he said, "I'm starved. Want to get something to eat?"

It was a minute before she made the transition from business to pleasure, and it was just as lucky she didn't have time to think about it. The less she thought, the less nervous she was. "Uh . . . sure."

He took her hand. "Come on. There's a place not far from here that has the best chowder on the coast."

Chowder sounded fine to Jessica, who couldn't deny the slight chill of the ocean air. Her jacket helped, as did his hand. It encircled hers in a grip that was firm and wonderfully warm.

The chowder was as good as he'd boasted it would be, though Jessica knew that some of its appeal, at least, came from the pier-front setting and the company. Along with the chowder, they polished off spinach salads and a small loaf of homemade wheat bread. Then they headed back to the car and made for the next stop on Carter's list.

Five stops—three for business, two for pleasure—and four hours later, they reached Harborside. As he'd done at each of the other projects they'd seen, Carter showed her around, giving her a brief history of the setting and how it had come to be developed, plus mention of his feelings about the experience. And as he'd done at each of the other projects, he stopped at the end to await her judgment.

"It's interesting," she said this time. "The concept— converting a mill into condominiums—limits things a little, but you've stretched those limits with the atrium. I love the atrium."

Carter felt as though he were coming to know her through her facial expressions alone, and her facial expression now, serious and somewhat analytical, told him that while she might admire the atrium, she certainly didn't love it. "It's okay, Jessica," he teased. He felt confident enough, based on her earlier reactions, to say, "You can be blunt."

She kept her eyes on the building, which was across the street from where they were standing. "I am being blunt. Given what you had to start with, this is really quite remarkable."

"Remarkable as in wildly exciting and dramatic?"

"Uh, not dramatic. Impressive."

"But you wouldn't want to live here."

"I didn't say that."

"Would you?"

Looking up, she caught the mischievous sparkle in his eye. It sparkled right through her in a way that something mischievous shouldn't have sparkled, but she didn't look away. She didn't want him to know how wonderfully warm he was making her feel by standing so close. "I think," she conceded a bit wryly, "that I'd rather live at Cadillac Cove."

"Or Riverside," he added, starting to grin in his own pleasure at the delightfully feminine flush on her cheeks. "Or the Sands."

"Or Walker Place," she tacked on, finishing the list of the places they'd visited. "Okay, this is my least favorite. But it's still good."

"Does that mean I have the job?"

Her brows flexed in an indulgent frown that came and went. "Of course, you have the job. Why do you ask?"

"Wasn't that the point of this trip—to see if you like my work?"

In truth, Jessica had forgotten that point, which surprised her, and in the midst of that surprise, she realized two things. First, she had already come to think of Carter as the architect of record. And second, she was enjoying herself and had been doing so from the time she'd first sat back in his car and decided to trust his driving. Somewhere, there, she'd forgotten to remember what a hellraiser he'd been once. She was thinking of him in terms of the present, and liking him. Did she like his work? "I like your work just fine."

His handsome mouth twitched in gentle amusement. "You could say it with a little enthusiasm."

Bewitched by that mouth and its small, subtle movements, she did as he asked. "I like your work just fine!"

"Really?"

"Really!"

The twitch at the corner of his mouth became a tentative grin. "Do you think I could do something good for Crosslyn Rise?"

"I think you could do something great for Crosslyn Rise!"

"You're not just saying that for old times' sake?"

Gazing up at him, she let out a laugh that was as easy as it was spontaneous. "If it were a matter of old times' sake, I'd have fired you long ago."

Behind the look in her eye, the sound of her laugh and the softness of her voice, Carter could have sworn he detected something akin to affection. Deeply touched by that thought, he took her chin in his hand. His fingers lightly caressed her skin, while his eyes searched hers for further sign of emotion. And he saw it. It was there. Yes, she liked him, and that made him feel even more victorious than when she'd said she liked his work. Unable to help himself, he moved his thumb over her mouth. When her lips parted, he ducked his head and replaced his thumb with his mouth.

His kiss was whisper light, one touch, then another, and Jessica couldn't have possibly stopped it. It felt too good, too real and far sweeter even than those heady kisses she'd dreamed about. But her body began to tremble—she didn't know whether in memory of the dream or in response to his kiss—and she was frightened.

"No," she whispered against his mouth. Her hands came up to grasp his jacket. "Please, Carter, no."

Lifting his head, Carter saw her fear. His body was telling him to kiss her again and deeper; his mind told him that he could do it and she'd capitulate. But his heart wasn't ready to push.

"I won't hurt you," he said softly.

"I know." Though her hands clutched his jacket, her eyes avoided his. "But I . . . don't want this."

I could make you want it, Carter thought, but he didn't say it, because it was typical of something the old Carter would say, and the last thing he wanted to do was to remind her of that. "Okay," he said softly, and took a step back, but only after he'd brushed his thumb over her cheek. Half turning from her, he took a deep breath, dug his fists into the pockets of his jacket and pursed his lips toward the mill that he'd redesigned. After a minute, when he'd regained control over his baser instincts, he sent her a sidelong glance.

"You like my work, and I like that. So a celebration's in order. What say we head back and have dinner at the Pagoda. Do you like Chinese food?"

Not trusting her voice, Jessica nodded.

"Want to try it?" he asked.

She nodded again.

Not daring to touch her, he chucked his chin in the direction of the car. "Shall we?"

To nod again would have seemed foolish even to her. So, tucking her hands into her pockets, she turned and headed for the car. By rights, she told herself, she ought to have pleaded the need to work and asked Carter to drive her home. She didn't for three reasons.

First, work could wait.

Second, she was hungry.

And third, she wasn't ready to have the day end.

6

THERE WAS A FOURTH REASON why Jessica agreed to have dinner with Carter. She wanted to show him that she could recover from his kiss, or was it herself that she wanted to show? It didn't matter, she supposed, because the end result was the same. She couldn't figure out why Carter had kissed her again, unless he'd seen in her eyes that she'd wanted him to, which she had. Since it wasn't wise for her to reinforce that impression, she had to carry on as though the kiss didn't matter.

It was easier said than done. Not only did the Pagoda have superb Chinese food, but it was elegantly served in a setting where the chairs were high backed and romantic, the drinks were fruity and potent, and the lights were low. None of that was conducive to remembering that she was there on business, that Carter's kisses most surely stemmed from either professional elation or personal arrogance, and that she didn't want or need anything from him but spectacular designs for Crosslyn Rise.

The atmosphere had *date* written all over it, and nothing Carter did dispelled that notion. He was a relaxed conversationalist, willing to talk about anything, from work to a television documentary they'd both seen, to the upcoming gubernatorial election. He drew her out in ways that she hadn't expected, got her thinking and talking about things she'd normally have felt beyond her ken. If she had stopped to remember where he'd come from, she'd have been amazed at the breadth and depth of his knowledge. But she didn't stop, because the man that he was obliterated images of the past. The man that he was held dominance over most everything, including, increasingly, her wariness of him as a man.

So her defenses were down by the time they returned to Crosslyn Rise. Darkness had fallen, lending an unreality to the scene, and while the drink had made her mellow, Carter had her intoxicated. That, added to her enjoyment of the evening, of the entire day, was why she gave no resistance when he slipped an arm around her as he walked her to the door. There, under the glow of the antique lamps, he took her chin again and tipped up her face.

"It's been a nice day," he told her in a voice that was low and male. "I'm glad you agreed to come with me, and not only to see the real estate. I've enjoyed the company."

She wanted to believe him enough to indulge in the fantasy for a few last minutes. "It has been nice," she agreed with a shy smile, feeling as though she could easily drown in the depths of his charcoal-brown eyes and be happy.

"The real estate? Or the company?"

"Both," was her soft answer.

He lowered his head and kissed her, touching her lips, caressing them for an instant before lifting his head again. "Was that as nice?"

It was a minute before she opened her eyes. "Mmm."

"I'd like to do it again."

"You thought it was nice, too?"

"If I didn't, I wouldn't want to do it again," he said with the kind of logic that no mind could resist, particularly one that was floating as lightly as Jessica's. "Okay?"

She nodded, and when he lowered his head this time, her lips were softer, more pliant than before. He explored their curves, opening them by small degrees until he could run his tongue along the inside. When she gasped, he drew back.

"It's all right," he whispered. He slid his arms around her, fitting her body to his. "I won't hurt you," he said when he felt the fine tremors that shook her. "Flow with it, Jessica. Let me try again."

That was just what he did, caressing innocently at first, deepening the kiss by stages until his tongue was playing at will along the inside of her mouth. She tasted fruity sweet, reminiscent of the drinks they'd had, and twice as heady. When his arms contracted to draw her even closer, he wasn't thinking as much about her trembling body as his own. He needed to feel the pressure of her breasts, of her belly and thighs, needed to feel all those feminine things against his hard, male body.

Jessica clung to his shoulders, overwhelmed by the fire he'd started within her. It was like her dream, but so much more real, with heat rushing through her veins, licking at nerve ends, settling in ultrasensitive spots. When Carter crushed her closer, then moved her body against his, she didn't protest, because she needed the friction, too. His hardness was a foil for her softness, a salve for the ache inside her.

But the salve was only good for a minute, and when the ache increased, she remembered her dream again. She'd had a similar ache in the dream—until her mind had sparked what was necessary to bring her release.

For a horrid split second, she feared that would happen again. Then the split second passed, and she struggled to regain control of herself. "Carter," she protested, dragging her mouth from his. Her palms went flat against his shoulders and pushed.

"It's okay," he said unevenly. "I won't hurt you."

"We have to stop."

It was another minute before his dark eyes focused. "Why? I don't understand."

Freeing herself completely, Jessica moved to the front door. She grasped the doorknob and leaned against the wood, taking the support from Crosslyn Rise that she'd taken from Carter moments before. "I'm not like that."

"Like what?"

"Easy."

Carter was having trouble thinking clearly. Either the throbbing of his body was interfering with his brain, or she was talking nonsense. "No one said you were easy. I was just kissing you."

"But it's not the first time. And you wanted more."

"Didn't you?" he blurted out before he could stop himself. And then he wasn't sorry, because the ache in his groin persisted, making him want to lash out at its cause.

Her eyes shot to his. "No. I don't sleep around."

"You wanted more. You were trembling for it. Be honest, Jessica. It won't kill you to admit it."

"It's not true."

"In a pig's eye," he muttered, and took a step back. Tipping his head the slightest bit, he studied her through narrowed lids. "What is it about me that you find so frightening? The fact that I'm the guy who made fun of you when we were kids, or the fact that I'm a guy, period."

"You don't frighten me."

"I can see it. I can see it in your eyes."

"Then you see wrong. I just don't want to go to bed with you. That's all."

"Why not?"

"Because."

"Because why? Come on, Jessica. You owe me an explanation. You've been leading me a merry chase all day, being just that little bit distant but closer than ever before. You've spent the better part of the day being a consummate tease—"

"I have not! I've just been me! I thought we were having a nice time. If I'd known there was a price to pay for that—" she fumbled in her purse for her keys "—I'd have been careful not to have enjoyed myself as much. Is sex part of your professional fee?"

Carter ran a hand through his hair, then dropped it to the tight muscles at the back of his neck. With the fading of desire came greater control, and with greater control, clearer thought. They were on the old, familiar road to name-calling, he knew, and that wouldn't accomplish a thing.

He held up a hand to signal a truce, then set about explaining it. In a very quiet voice, he said, "Let's get one thing straight. I want you because you turn me on."

"That's—"

"Shh. Let me finish." When she remained silent, he said even more slowly, "You turn me on. No strings attached. No price I expect you to pay for lunch or dinner. You...just...turn me on. I didn't expect it, and I don't want it, because you *are* a client and I don't get involved with clients. It's not the way I work. Sex has nothing to do with payments of any kind. It has to do with two people liking each other, respecting each other, then being attracted to each other. It has to do with two people being close, but needing to be even closer. It has to do with two people wanting to know each other in ways that other people don't." He paused to take a breath. "That was what I wanted just now. It was what I've been wanting all day."

Jessica didn't know what to answer. If she'd been madly in love with a man, she couldn't have hoped for a sweeter explanation. But she wasn't madly in love with Carter, which had to be why she was having trouble believing in the sincerity of his desire.

"As for sleeping around," Carter went on in that same quiet voice, "it means having indiscriminate sex with lots of different people. I'm not involved with anyone else right now. I haven't been intimately involved with anyone for a while. And I feel like I know you better than I've known any woman in years. So if I took you to bed, I wouldn't be sleeping around. And neither would you, unless you've been with others—"

She shook her head so vigorously that he dropped that particular line of inquiry. He'd known it wasn't true anyway. "Have you been with anyone since your husband?"

She shook her head more slowly this time.

"Before him?"

She shook her head a third time.

"Was it unpleasant with him?" Carter asked, but he knew that he'd made a mistake the minute the words were out. Jessica bowed her head and concentrated on fitting the key to the lock. "Don't go," he said quickly, but she opened the door and stepped inside.

"I can't talk about this," she murmured.

He took a step forward. "Then we'll talk about something else."

"No. I have to go."

"Talk of sex doesn't have to make you uncomfortable."

"It does. It's not something two strangers discuss."

"We're not strangers."

She looked up at him. "We are in some ways. You're more experienced than me. You won't be able to understand what I feel."

"Try me, and we'll see."

She shook her head, said softly, "I have to go," and slowly closed the door.

For a second before the latch clicked in place, Carter was tempted to resist. But the second passed, and the opportunity was gone. Short of banging the knocker or ringing the bell, he was cut off from her.

It was just as well. She needed time to get used to the idea of wanting him. He could give her that, he supposed.

HE GAVE HER NEARLY AN HOUR, which was how long it took him to drive back to Boston, change clothes and make a pot of coffee. Then he picked up the phone and called her.

Her voice sounded calm and professional. "Hello?"

"Hi, Jessica. It's me. I just wanted to make sure you're okay."

She was silent for a minute. Then she said in the same composed voice, "I'm fine."

"You're not angry, are you?"

"No."

"Good." He paused. "I didn't mean any harm by asking what I did." He tapped a finger on the lip of his coffee cup. "I'm just curious." He looked up at the ceiling. "You're afraid of me. I keep trying to figure out why."

"I'm not afraid of you," came her quiet voice, sounding less confident than before.

"Then why won't you let yourself go when I kiss you?"

"Because I'm not the letting-go type."

"I think you could be. I think you want to be."

"I want to be exactly what I am right now. I'm not unhappy with my life, Carter. I'm doing what I like with people I like. If that wasn't so, I'd have changed things. But I like my life. I really like my life. You seem to think that I'm yearning for something else, but I'm not. I'm perfectly content."

Carter thought she was being a little too emphatic and a little too repetitive. He had the distinct feeling she was making the point to herself as much as to him, which meant that she wasn't as sure of her needs as she claimed, and that suited him just fine.

"You're not content about Crosslyn Rise," he reminded her, then hurried on, "which is another reason I'm calling. I'm going to start making some preliminary sketches, but I'll probably want to come to walk around again. I'd like to take some pictures—of the house, the land, possible building sites, the oceanfront. They're all outside pictures, so you don't have to be there, but I didn't want to go wandering around without your permission."

"You have my permission."

"Great. Why don't I give you a call when I have something to show you?"

"That sounds good." She paused. "Carter?"

He held his breath. "Yes?"

After a brief hesitation, her voice came. This time it sounded neither professional nor insecure, but sincere. "Thanks again for today. It really was nice."

He let out the breath and smiled. "My pleasure. Talk with you soon."

"Uh-huh."

WHAT TIME JESSICA SPENT at home that week, she spent looking out the window. Or it seemed that way. She made excuses for herself—she was restless reading term papers, she needed exercise, she could use the time to think—but she managed to wander from room to room, window to window, glancing nonchalantly out each one. Her eyes were anything but nonchalant, searching the landscape for Carter on the chance that either she'd missed his car on the driveway or he'd parked out of sight.

She saw no sign of him, which mean that either he'd come while she was in Cambridge or he hadn't come at all.

Nor did he call. She imagined that he might have tried her once or twice while she was out, and for the first time in her life she actually considered buying an answering machine. But that was in a moment of weakness. She didn't like answering machines. And besides, it would be worse to have an answering machine and not receive a message, than to not have one and wonder. Where one could wonder, one had hope.

And that thought confused her, because she wasn't sure why she wanted hope. Carter Malloy was . . . Carter Malloy. They were involved with each other on a professional basis, but that was all. Yes, she'd enjoyed spending Sunday with him. She'd begun to realize just how far he'd come as a person in the years she'd known him. And she did hope, she supposed, that there might be another Sunday or two like that.

But nothing sexual was ever going to happen between them. He wasn't her type—a perfect example being his failure to call. In Jessica's book, when a man was romantically interested in a woman, he didn't leave her alone for days. He called her, stopped in to see her, left messages at the office. Carter certainly could have done that, but there had been no message from him among the pink slips the department secretary had handed her that week.

He was showing his true colors, she decided. Despite all his sweet talk—sex talk—he wasn't really interested in her, which didn't surprise her in the least. He was a compelling man. Sex appeal oozed from him. She, on the other hand, had no sex appeal at all. Her genes had been generous in certain fields, but sex appeal wasn't one.

So what did Carter want with her? She didn't understand the motive behind his kisses, and the more she tried to, the more frustrated she became. The only thing she could think was that he was having a kind of perverse fun with her, and that hurt. It hurt, because one part of her liked him, respected him personally and professionally and found him sexy as all get out. It would be far easier, she realized, to admire him from a distance, than to let him come close and show her just how unsatisfying she was to a man.

Knowing that the more she brooded, the worse it would be, Jessica kept herself as busy as possible. Rather than wander from window to window at home, by midweek she was spending as much time as possible at school. Work, like Poppycock, had a soothing effect on her, and there was work aplenty to do. When she wasn't grading exams, she was reading term papers or working with one of the two students for whom she was a dissertation advisor. And the work was uplifting—which didn't explain why, when she returned to Crosslyn Rise Friday evening, she felt distinctly let down. She'd never had that experience before. Work had always been a bellwether for her mood. She decided that she was simply tired.

So she slept late on Saturday morning, staying in bed until nine, dallying over breakfast, taking a leisurely shower, though she had nothing but laundry and local errands and more grading to do. She didn't pay any heed to the windows, knowing that Carter wouldn't come on a Saturday. Work was work. He'd be there during the week, preferably when she wasn't around. Which was just as well, as far as she was concerned.

It was therefore purely by accident that, with her arms loaded high with sheets to be laundered, she came down the back steps and caught a glimpse of something shiny and blue out the landing window. Heart thundering, she came to an abrupt halt, stared out at the driveway and swallowed hard.

He'd come. On a Saturday. When she was wearing jeans and a sweatshirt pushed up to the elbows, looking like one of her students playing laundress. But someone had to do the laundry, she thought a bit frantically; the days of having Annie Malloy to help with it were long gone.

Ah, the irony of it, she mused. Then the back bell rang, and she ceased all musings. Panicked, she glanced at her sweatshirt, then at the linens in her arms, then down the stairs toward the door. If she didn't answer it, he'd think she wasn't home.

That would be the best thing.

But she couldn't do it. Tucking the sheets into a haphazard ball, she ran down the stairs, crossed through the back vestibule and opened the door to Carter.

His appearance did nothing to ease her breathlessness. Wearing jeans and a plaid flannel shirt, he looked large and masculine. His clothes were comfortably worn—a far cry from the last time she'd seen him in jeans, when they'd been dirty and torn—and fit his leanly muscled legs like a glove. The shirt was rolled to the elbow, much as her sweatshirt was, only his forearms were sinewy, spattered with dark hair, striped on the inside with the occasional vein. His collar was open, showing off the strength of his neck and shoulders, and from one of those shoulders hung a camera.

"Hi," she said. In an attempt to curb her breathlessness, she put a hand to her chest. "How are you?"

He was just fine, now that he was here. All week he'd debated about when to stop by; he couldn't remember when he'd given as much thought to anything. Except her. She'd been on his mind a lot. Now he knew why. Looking at her, taking in the casual way she was dressed, the oversized pink sweatshirt and the faded blue jeans that clung to slender legs, he felt relieved. Her features, too, did that to him. She was perfectly unadorned—long hair shiny clean and drawn into a high ponytail, skin free of makeup and healthy looking, smile small but bright, glasses sliding down the bridge of her nose—but she looked wonderful. She was a breath of fresh air, he decided, finally putting his finger on one of the things he most liked about her. She was different from the women he'd known. She was natural and unpretentious. She was refreshing.

"I'm real fine," he drawled with a lazy smile. "Just stoppin' in to disturb your Saturday morning." His gaze touched on the bundle she held.

Wrapping both arms around the linens, she hugged them to her. "I, uh, always use Saturdays for this. Usually I'm up earlier. I should have had two washes done by now. I slept late."

"You must have been tired." He searched for shadows under her eyes, but either her glasses hid them, or they just weren't there. Her skin was clear, unmottled by fatigue, a smooth blend of ivory and pink. "It's been a busy week?"

"Very," she said with a sigh and a smile.

"Will you be able to relax this weekend?"

"A little. I still have more work to do, but then there are things like this—" she nodded toward the linens "—and the market and the drugstore, none of which are heavily intellectual tasks. I relax when I do those."

"No time to sit back, put your feet up and vegetate?"

She shook her head. "I'm not good at vegetating."

"I used to be good at it, back in the days when I was raising hell." His mouth took on a self-effacing twist. "Used to drive my mother wild. Whenever the police showed up at the door, she knew she'd find me sprawled out in the back room watching TV." The twist gentled. "I don't have much time for vegetating now, either—" he jabbed his chin toward the camera "—which is why I'm here. I thought I'd do that exploring. I have nothing to think about but Crosslyn Rise, and it's a gorgeous day." He made a quick decision, based on the open look on her face. "Want to come?"

Nothing seemed to be helping Jessica's breathlessness or the incessant fluttering of her insides. Suddenly she didn't seem to be able to make a decision, either. "I don't know...there's this laundry to do...and vacuuming." She could feel the warm air coming in past him, and it beckoned. "I ought to dust . . . and you'll probably be able to think more creatively if I'm not around."

"I'd like the company. And I won't talk if the creative mode hits. Come on. Just for a little while. It's too special a day to miss."

His eyes weren't as much charcoal brown today, she decided, as milk chocolatey, and their lashes seemed absurdly thick. Had she never noticed that before?

"Uh, I have so much to do," she argued, but meekly.

"Tell you what," Carter said. "I'll start out and follow the same route we took last time. You take care of what you have to, then join me."

That sounded like a fair compromise to Jessica. If he was willing to be flexible, she couldn't exactly remain rigid. Besides, Saturday or not, he was working on her project. Maybe he wanted to bounce ideas off her. "I may be a little while," she cautioned.

"No sweat. I'll be here longer than that. Take your time." With a wink, he set off.

The wink set her back a good ten minutes. Several of those were spent with her back against the wall by the door, trying to catch up with her racing pulse. Several more were spent wandering through the kitchen into the den, before she realized that she was supposed to be headed for the laundry, which was in the basement. The rest were spent getting the washer settings right, normally a simple task, now complicated by a sorely distracted mind.

Never in her life had she done the vacuuming as quickly as she did then. It was nervous energy, she told herself, and that reasoning held on through a dusting job that probably stirred more than it gathered. Fortunately, the rooms in question were only those few she used on a regular basis, which meant that she was done in no time. The bed linens were in the dryer and her personal things in the wash when she laced on a pair of sneakers, grabbed a half-filled bag of bread and slipped out the door.

Carter was sitting cross-legged on the warm grass by the duck pond. Though for all intents and purposes he was concentrating on the antics of the ducks, he'd kept a lookout for her arrival. The sight of her brought the warm feeling it always did, plus something akin to excitement—which was amusing, since in the old days he'd have labeled her the least exciting person in the world. But that was in the old days, at a time in his life when he'd appreciated precious little, certainly nothing subtle and mature, which were the ways in which he found Jessica exciting. He could never have appreciated her intellect, the way she thought through issues, the natural curiosity that had her listening to things he said and asking questions. She was a thoroughly stimulating companion, even in silence—unless she felt threatened. When that happened, she was as dogmatic and closed minded as he'd once thought her to be.

The key, of course, was to keep her from feeling threatened. Most of the time, that was easy, particularly since he felt increasingly protective of her. The times when it was difficult almost always had to do with sex, which was when he was at his least controlled both physically and emotionally.

But he'd try. He'd try, because the prize was worth it.

"Watch out for the muck!" he called, and watched her give wide berth to a spot of ground that hadn't quite dried out from the spring thaw. His eyes followed her as she approached, one hand tucked into the pocket of her jeans, her ponytail swaying gently with her step. "That was fast."

"Don't you know it," she said in a way that stunned him, then pleased him in the next breath. She'd drawled the words. Yes, there was self-mockery in them, but there was playfulness, too. Opening the bag of bread, she began breaking off chunks and tossing them toward the ducks, who quacked their appreciation. "I hate cleaning. I do it dutifully. But I hate it."

"You should hire someone—and don't tell me you can't afford it. That kind of help is cheap."

But she nixed the idea with the scrunch of her nose, which served the double purpose of hitching her glasses up. "There's really not enough to do." She tossed out another handful of bread and watched the ducks try to out-waddle each other to where it landed. "I hire a crew twice a year to do the parts of the house that I don't use, but there's no good reason why I can't do the rest myself." She turned to stare at him hard, but her voice was too gentle to be accusing. "Unless someone stands at my door tempting me with the best spring weather that's come along so far." She looked around, took a deep breath, didn't pause to wonder whether the exhilaration she felt was from the air or not. She was tired of wondering about things like that. She was too analytical. For once, she wanted to—what was it he'd said—go with the flow. "So," she said, reaching for more bread, "are you being inspired?"

"Here? Always. It's a beautiful spot." Tossing several feathers out of the way, he patted the grass by his side.

She sat down and shot a look at the camera that lay in his lap. It wasn't one of the instant models, but the real thing. "Have you used it?"

He nodded. "I've taken pictures of the house, the front lawn and the beach. Not here, yet. I'm just sitting."

She aimed a handful of bread crumbs toward the ducks. "Are you a good photographer?"

"I'm competent. I get the shots I need, but they're practical, rather than artistic." He took the camera up, made several shifts in the settings, raised it to his eye and aimed it at her.

She held up a hand to block the shot and turned her head away. "I hate having my picture taken even more than I hate cleaning!"

"Why?"

"I don't like being focused on." She dared a glance at him, relaxing once she saw that he'd put the camera back down.

"Focused on" could be interpreted both broadly and narrowly. Carter had the feeling that both applied in Jessica's case. "Why not?" he asked, bemused.

"Because it's embarrassing. I'm not photogenic."

"I don't believe that."

"It's true. The camera exaggerates every flaw. I have plenty without the exaggeration."

Looking at her, with the sun glancing off her hair and a blush of self-consciousness on her cheeks, Carter could only think of how pretty she was. "What flaws do you have?"

"Come on, Carter—"

"Tell me." The quacking of the ducks seemed to second his command.

Sure that he was ridiculing her, she studied his eyes. She saw no teasing there, though, only challenge, and where Carter challenged her, she was conditioned to respond. "I'm plain. Totally and utterly plain. My face is too thin, my nose is too small, and my eyes are boring."

He stared at her. "Boring? Are you kidding? And there's nothing wrong with the shape of your face or your nose. Do you have any idea what a pleasure it is for me to look at you after having to look at other women all week?" At her blank look, he said, "You've grown up well, Jessica. You may have felt plain as a child, but you're not a child anymore, and what you think of as plainness is straightforward, refreshing good looks."

Her blankness had yielded to incredulity. "Why do you say things like that?"

"Because they're true!"

"I don't believe it for a minute," she said. It seemed the only way to cope with the awkwardness she felt. Rising to her feet, she tossed the last of the bread from the bag and set off. "You're just trying to butter me up so I'll like your designs." Wadding up the bag, she stuffed it into a pocket.

Carter was after her in a minute, gently catching her ponytail to draw her up short as he overtook her. His body was a solid wall before her, his hand in her hair a smaller but no less impenetrable wall behind. Against her temple, his breath was a warm sough of emotion. "If I wanted to butter you up, I'd just do my work and mind my own business about the rest. But I can't do it—any more than I can sit back and listen to you denigrate yourself. I'm highly attracted to you. Why can't you believe that?"

Struck as always by his closeness, Jessica's breathing had quickened. Her eyes were lowered, focusing on his shirt, and though there was nothing particularly sensual about the plaid, there was something decidedly so about the faintly musky scent of his skin.

"I'm not the kind of women men find highly attractive," she explained in a small voice.

"Is that another gem of wisdom from your ex-husband?"

"No. It's something I've deduced after thirty-three years of observation. I don't turn heads. I never have and never will."

"The women who turn heads—the sharp lookers, the fashion plates—aren't the women men want. Call it macho, but they want softer women. You're a softer woman. And I want you."

"But you have your choice of the best women in the city."

"And I choose you. Doesn't that tell you anything?"

"It tells me that you're going through a phase. Let's call it—" she raised her eyes to his to make her point "—the give-the-little-lady-a-thrill-for-old-times'-sake phase."

Dangerously close to anger, Carter drew her closer until she was flush against him. "That's insulting, Jessica." His dark eyes blazed into hers. "Can't you give me a little credit for honesty? Have I ever lied to you?" When she didn't answer, he did it for her. "No. I may have said cruel things, or downright wrong things, but they were the things I was honestly feeling at the time. We've already established that I was a bastard. But at least give me credit for honesty."

His blood was pulsing more thickly as her curves imprinted themselves on his body. "I've been honest with words. And I've been honest with this." He captured her mouth before she could open hers to protest, and he kissed her with an ardor that could have been from hunger or anger.

Jessica didn't know which. All she knew was that her defenses fell in less time than ever before, that she couldn't have kept her mouth stiff if she'd tried, that she should have been shocked when his tongue surged into her mouth, but the only source of shock was her own enjoyment.

That thought, though, came a moment too soon, because she was in for another small shock. Well before she was ready, he ended the kiss. She hadn't even begun to gather her wits when he took her hand from its stranglehold of his shirt and lowered it to the straining fly of his jeans.

"No way," he said hoarsely, "no way could I fake that." Keeping his hand over hers, he molded her fingers to his shape, pressing her palm flat, manipulating it in a rubbing motion. A low sound slipped from his throat as he pressed his lips to her neck.

Jessica was stunned by the extent of his arousal, then stunned again when the heat of it seemed to increase. Her breathing was short and scattered, but Carter's was worse, and a fine quaking simmered in the muscles of his arms and legs.

No, he couldn't fake what she felt, and the knowledge was heady. It made her feel soft and feminine and eager to know more of the strength beneath her hand. Without conscious thought, she began to stroke him. Her eyes closed. Her head tipped to give his mouth access to her throat. Her free arm stole to the bunched muscles of his back. And when she became aware of a restlessness between her legs, she arched toward him.

Carter made a low, guttural sound. Wrenching her hand from him, he wrapped her in his arms and crushed her close, then closer still. "Don't move," he warned in a voice that was more sand than substance. "Don't move. Give me a minute. A minute."

The trembling went on as he held her tight, but Jessica wasn't sure how much of it was her own. Weak-kneed and shaky, she was grateful that his convulsive hold was keeping her upright. Without it, she'd surely have slid down to the grass and begged him to take her there, which was precisely what the tight knot at the pit of her stomach demanded.

That was probably the biggest shock of all. The dream she could reason away. She could attribute it to any number of vague things. But when she was being held in Carter's arms, when she felt every hard line of his body and not only took pleasure in the hardness but hungered to have it deeper inside her, she couldn't lie to herself any longer.

The issue, of course, was what to make of the intense desire she felt for him. The moment would pass now, she knew. Once Carter regained control of his libido, he would set her back, perhaps take her hand and lead her on through the woods. He might talk, ask her what she feared, try to get her to admit to his desire and to her own, but he wouldn't force her into anything she didn't want.

It wasn't that she didn't want sex with Carter, rather that she wasn't ready for it. She'd never been a creature of impulse. It was one thing to "go with the flow" and spurn housekeeping chores in favor of a walk on the woods, quite another to "go with the flow" and expose herself, body and soul, to a man. She'd done that once and been hurt, and though she'd never made vows of chastity, the memory of that hurt kept her shy of sex.

If she was ever to make love with Carter, she had to understand exactly what she was doing and why. She also had to decide whether the risk was worth it.

7

CARTER DIDN'T LEAVE right away. Nor did he allow Jessica to leave. He insisted she stay while he took the pictures he needed at the duck pond, then walked her back to the house. She had feared he'd want to talk about what had happened, but either he was as surprised by its power as she, or he sensed she wasn't ready. He said nothing about the kiss, about the way she'd touched him, or about the fact that he'd nearly lost it there and then in front of the ducks.

Instead, he sent her inside to finish her chores while he completed his own outside. Then he drove her to the supermarket and walked up and down the aisles with her, tossing the occasional unusual item into her cart. When they returned to Crosslyn Rise, he made his special tuna salad, replete with diced water chestnuts and red pepper relish.

After lunch, he left.

HE CALLED ON MONDAY evening to say that the photos he'd taken had come out well and that he was getting down to some serious sketching.

He called on Thursday evening to say that he was pleased with the progress he was making and would she be free on Sunday afternoon to take a look at what he'd drawn.

She was free, of course. The semester's work was over, exams and papers graded, grades duly recorded—which was wonderful in the sense of freeing her up, lousy in the sense of giving her more time to think. The thinker in her decided that she definitely wanted to see what he'd drawn, but she didn't trust him—or herself—to have a show-and-tell meeting at Crosslyn Rise.

So they arranged to meet at Carter's office, which satisfied Jessica's need on several scores. First, she was curious to see more of him in his professional milieu. Second, even if he kissed her, and even if she responded, the setting was such that nothing could come of it.

She guessed she was curious to see him, period. It had been a long week since the Saturday before, a long week of replaying what had happened, of feeling the excitement again, of imagining an even deeper involvement. Though it still boggled her mind, she had to accept that he did want her. The evidence had been conclusive. She still didn't know *why* he wanted her, and the possibilities were diverse, running from the wildly exciting to the devastating. But that was another reason why the setting suited her purpose. It was safe. She could see him, get to know him better, but she wouldn't have to take a stand on the physical side of the issue.

And then, there was Crosslyn Rise. The part of her that had acclimated itself to the conversion of the Rise was anxious to see what he'd drawn. That part wanted to get going, to decide on an architectural plan, have it formally drawn up and give it to Gordon so that he could enlist his investors. That part of Jessica wanted to act before its counterpart backed out.

Jessica wasn't sure what she'd expected when she took a first look at Carter's drawings, but it certainly wasn't the multicolored spread before her. Yes, there were pencil sketches on various odd pieces of paper, but he'd taken the best of those ideas and converted them into something that could well have been a polished promotion for the place.

"Who drew these?" she asked, slightly awed.

"I did." There were times when he left such drawings to project managers, but he'd wanted to do this himself. When it came to Crosslyn Rise, he was the project manager, and he didn't give a damn whether his partner accused him of ill-using the resources at hand. Crosslyn Rise was his baby from start to finish, even if it meant late nights such as the ones he'd put in this week. They were worth it. Concentrating on his work was better than concentrating on his need.

"But this is art. I never pictured anything like this."

"It's called a presentation," he said dryly. "The idea is to snow the client right off the bat."

"Well, I'm snowed."

"By the presentation, maybe, but do you like what's in it?"

At first glance, she did. At his caveat, she took a closer look, moving one large sheet aside to look at the next.

"I've drawn the main house in cross sections, as I envision it looking once all the work is done," he explained, "and a head-on view of the condo cluster at the duck pond. Since the clusters will all be based on the same concept, a variation on the Georgian theme, I wanted to try out one cluster on you first."

Her eyes were glued to the drawing. "It's incredible."

"Is it what you imagined?"

"No. It looks more Cape-ish than Georgian. But it's real. More modern. Interesting."

He wasn't sure if "interesting" was good or bad, but when he asked, she held up a hand and studied the drawing in silence for several minutes. "Interesting," she repeated, but there was a warmth in the word. Then she smiled. "Nice."

Carter basked in her smile, which was some consolation for the fact that he wanted to hug her but didn't dare. Not only did he sense that she wasn't ready for more hugs, but he feared that if he touched her, office or no, he wouldn't be able to stop this time. As it was, her smile, which was so rare, did dangerous things to him.

He cleared his throat. "Obviously this is rough. But I wanted to convey the general idea." He touched a lean finger to one area, then another. "The roof angle here is what reminds you of a Cape. It can be modified, but it allows for skylights. Today's market loves skylights." His finger shifted. "I've deliberately scaled down the pillars and balconies so that they don't compete with the main house. The main house should set the tone for stateliness. The clusters can echo it, but they ought to be more subtle. I want them to nestle into their surroundings. In some ways the focus of the clusters *is* those surroundings."

Jessica cast a sideways glance at him. He had a long arm propped straight on the drafting table and was close enough to touch, close enough to smell, close enough to want. Ignoring the last and the buzzing that played havoc with her insides, she said, "I think you're hung up on those surroundings."

"Me?" His dark eyes shone with indulgence one moment, vehemence the next. "No way. At least, not enough that it would color my better judgment. And my better judgment tells me that people will buy at Crosslyn Rise for the setting, nearly as much as for the nuts and bolts of what they're getting. Which isn't to say that we can skimp on those nuts and bolts." Again he referred to the drawing, tracing sweeping lines with his finger. "I've angled each of the units differently, partly for interest, partly for privacy. Either you and Gordon—or if you want to wait, the consortium—will have to decide on the size of the units. Personally, I'd hate to do anything less than a three bedroom setup. People usually want more space rather than less."

Jessica hadn't thought that far. "The person to speak with about that might be Nina Stone. She's a broker. She'd have a feel for what people in this area want."

"Do I know Nina Stone?" Carter asked, trying to place the name.

"She knew you," Jessica replied, wondering whether the two of them would hit it off and not sure she liked that idea. "Or rather, she knew *of* you. Your reputation precedes you."

Once he'd left New York, Carter had worked long and hard to establish himself and his name. "That's gratifying."

"Uh-huh. She already has you pegged as a ruggedly masculine individual."

Which wasn't the most professional of assessments, he mused. "You discussed me with her?"

"I mentioned we were working together."

He nodded his understanding, but, to Jessica's selfish delight, had no particular interest in knowing more about Nina. His finger was back on the drawing, this time tapping his rendition of the duck pond. "We may run into a problem with water. The land in this area is wetter than in the others. When we reach the point of having the backers lined up, I'll have a geological specialist take a look."

"Could the problem be serious?"

"Nah. It shouldn't be more than a matter of shifting the clusters to the right or the left, and I want them set back anyway so the ducks won't be disturbed. The main house draws water from its own wells. I'm assuming the condos would do the same, but an expert could tell us more on that, too."

Up to that point, Jessica had been aware of only two problems—coming to terms with the sale of Crosslyn Rise, and dealing with Carter Malloy. Now, mention of a possible water problem brought another to mind. "What if we can't get enough backers?"

Surprised by the question, he shot her a look. Her eyes were wide with concern. "To invest in the project? We'll get enough."

"Will we? You've had more experience in this kind of thing than I have. Is there a chance we'll come up with plans that no one will support?"

"It's not probable."

"But is it possible?"

"Anything's possible. It's possible that the economy will crash at ten past ten tomorrow morning, but it's no more probable that it will happen than that Gordon won't be able to find the backers we need." He paused, sliding his gaze over her face. "You're really worried?"

"I haven't been. I haven't thought about it much at all, but suddenly here you are with exciting drawings, and the project seems very real. I'd hate to go through all this and then have the whole thing fizzle."

Throwing caution to the winds, he did put his arm around her then. "It won't. Trust me. It won't."

The confidence in his voice, even more so than the words, was what did it. That, and the support his body offered. For the first time, she truly felt as though Carter shared the responsibility of Crosslyn Rise with her, and while a week or two before, that thought would have driven her wild, she was comfortable with it now. She'd come a long way.

"I have theater tickets for Thursday night," came Carter's low voice. "Come with me."

Taken totally off guard, she didn't know what to say.

His breath was warm on her hair. "Do you have other plans?"

"No."

"They're for *Cat on a Hot Tin Roof*."

Tipping her head, she looked up at him. "You got tickets," she breathed in awe, because she'd been trying to get them for weeks without success. But going to the theater with Carter was a *date*.

"Will you come?"

"I don't know," she said a bit helplessly. Everything physical about him lured her, as did, increasingly, everything else about him. He was so good to be with. The problem, as always, lay with her.

"If you won't, I'm giving the tickets back. There's no one else I want to take, and I don't want to go alone."

"That's blackmail," she argued.

"Not blackmail. Just a chance to see the hottest revival of the decade."

"I know, I know," she murmured, weakening. It was easy to do that when someone as strong as Carter was offering support.

"The semester's over. What better way to celebrate?"

"I have to be at school all day Thursday planning for the summer term."

"But the pressure's off. So before it's on again, have a little fun. You deserve it."

She wasn't as concerned with what she deserved as with what going on a date with Carter would mean. It would mean a shift in their relationship, a broadening of it. Going on a date with Carter would mean being with him at night in a crowded theater, perhaps alone before or after. All kinds of things could happen. She wasn't sure she was ready.

Then again, she wasn't sure she could resist.

"Come on, Jessica. I really want to go."

So do I, Jessica thought. Her eyes fell to his mouth. She liked looking at his mouth. "I'd have to meet you there."

"Why can't I pick you up?" he asked, and the corners of that mouth turned down.

"Because I don't know exactly where I'll be."

"You could call me at the office and let me know. It's only a ten-minute drive to Cambridge."

Her eyes met his. "More in traffic. And it's silly for you to go back and forth like that."

"I want to go back and forth." If he was taking her out for the evening, he wanted to do it right. Besides, he didn't like the idea of her traveling alone.

Jessica, though, was used to traveling alone. More than that, she was determined to keep things light and casual. It was the only way she could handle the thought of a date with Carter. "Tell me where to meet you and when. I'll be there."

"Why are you being so stubborn?" he asked. In the next breath, he relented. "Sorry. Six-thirty at the Sweetwater Café."

"I thought *Cat on a Hot Tin Roof* was at the Colonial." She knew very well it was—and what he was trying to do.

His naughty eyes didn't deny it. "The Sweetwater Café is close by. We can get something to eat there before the show." When she looked momentarily skeptical, he said, "You have to eat, Jessica." When still she hesitated, he added, "Indulge me. I'm letting you meet me there, which I don't like. So at least let me feed you first."

Looking up into his dark eyes, she came to an abrupt realization. It was no longer a matter of not being sure. She

couldn't resist—not when he had an arm draped so pro-
tectively across her shoulders, not when he was looking
at her so intently, not when she wanted both to go on forever and ever. He made her feel special. Cared for. Feminine. She doubted, at that minute, that she'd have been
able to refuse him a thing.

SO SHE AGREED. Naturally she had second thoughts, but
after a day of suffering through those, she lost patience
with herself. Since she'd agreed to go out with Carter, she
told herself, she was going, and since she was going, she
intended to make the most of it. She had her share of pride,
and that pride dictated that she do everything in her power
to make sure Carter didn't regret having asked her out.

He didn't regret it so far, at least; he called her each night
just to say hello. But talking on the phone or having a
business meeting or even driving north on a Sunday was
different from going out at night to something that had
nothing to do with work. She wanted to look good.

To that end, she arranged to finish up with work by two
on Thursday. The first stop she made then was to the boutique where she'd bought the sweater she'd worn to Maine;
if stylish had worked once, she figured it would work
again. But stylish in that shop was funky, which wasn't her
style at all. She was about to give up hope when the owner
brought a dress from the back that was perfect. A lime-
green sheath of silk that was self-sashed and fell to just
above the knee, it was sleeveless and had a high turtleneck that draped her neck in the same graceful way that
the rest of the fabric draped her body. The dress was feminine without being frilly. She felt special enough in it not
to look at the price tag, and by the time she had to write
out a check, she was committed enough to it not to mind
the higher-than-normal cost.

Her second stop was at a shoe store, where she picked up a pair of black patent leather heels and a small bag to match.

Her third stop was at Mario's. Mario had been doing her hair—a blunt cut to keep the ends under control—bi-monthly for several years, and for the first time she allowed him more freedom. Enhancing her own natural wave with rollers and a heat lamp, he gave her a look that was softer and more stylish than anything she'd ever worn. As the icing on the cake, he caught one side high over her ear with a pearl clip. The look pleased Jessica so much that she left the salon, went to the jewelry store next door and splurged on a pair of pearl earrings to match the clip. Then she returned to her office, where she'd left cosmetics and stockings.

The day had been warm and humid, as late spring days often were, and when Jessica left Harvard, retrieved her car and set off for Boston, dull gray clouds were dotting the sky. She barely noticed. Her thoughts were on the way she looked and the comments she'd drawn from the few of her colleagues she'd happened to pass as she left. They had done double takes, which either said she looked really good, or so different from how she usually looked that they couldn't believe it was her.

She couldn't quite believe it was her. For one thing, the fact that she liked the way she looked was a first. For another, the fact that she was heading for a date with a man like Carter Malloy was incredible. Unable to reconcile either, given that her nerves were jangling with excitement, she half decided that it wasn't her in the car at all, but another woman. That thought brought a silly grin to her face.

The grin faded, but the excitement didn't. It was over-shadowing her nervousness by the time she parked in the

garage under the Boston Common, and by the time she
emerged onto the Common itself and realized that she was
at the corner farthest from where she as going, she was
feeling too high to mind. Her step was quick, in no way
slowed by the unfamiliarity of the new heels.

What gave her pause, though, were the drops of rain
that, one by one, in slow succession, began to hit her. They
were large and warm. She looked worriedly at the sky, not
at all reassured by the ominous cloud overhead or the blue
that surrounded it in too distant a way. Furious at herself
for not having brought an umbrella, she walked faster. She
could beat the rain, she decided, but she wished she'd
parked closer.

To her dismay, the drops grew larger, came harder and
more often. She broke into a half run, holding her hand-
bag over her head, looking around for shelter. But there
was none. Trees were scattered on either side of the paved
walks, but they were of the variety whose branches were
too high to provide any shelter at all.

For a split second she stopped and looked frantically
back at the entrance to the parking garage, but it seemed
suddenly distant, separated from her by a million thick
raindrops. If she returned there, she'd be farther than ever
from the Sweetwater Café—and drenched anyway.

So she ran faster, but within minutes, the rain reached
downpour proportions. She was engulfed as much by it
as by disbelief. Other people rushed along, trying to protect themselves as she was, but she paid them no heed. All
she could think of was the beautiful green silk dress that
was growing wetter by the minute, the painstakingly
styled hair that was growing wilder by the minute, the
shiny black shoes that were growing more speckled by the
minute.

Panicked, she drew up under a large-trunked tree in the hope that something, *anything* would be better than nothing. But as though to mock her, the rain began to come sideways. When she shifted around the tree, it shifted, too. Horrified at what was happening but helpless to stop it, she looked from side to side for help but there was none. She was caught in the worst kind of nightmare.

Unable to contain it, she cried out in frustration, then cried out again when the first one didn't help. The second didn't, either, and she felt nearly as much a fool for making it as for standing there in the rain. So she started off again, running as fast as she could given that her glasses were streaked with rain, her shoes were soaked and her heart felt like lead.

It was still pouring when she finally turned down the alley that led to the Sweetwater Café. As the brick walkway widened into a courtyard, she slowed her step. Rushing was pointless. There was nothing the rain could do to her that it already hadn't. She couldn't possibly go to the theater with Carter. The evening was ruined. All that was left was to tell him, return to her car and drive home.

Shortly before she reached the café's entrance, her legs betrayed her. Stumbling to the nearby brick wall, she leaned her shoulder against it, covered her face with her hands and began to cry.

That was how Carter found her, as he came from the opposite end of the courtyard. He wasn't sure it was her at first; he hadn't expected such a deep green dress, such a wild array of hair or nearly so much leg. But as he slowed his own step, he sensed the familiar in the defeated way she stood. His insides went from hot to cold in the few seconds it took him to reach her side.

"Jessica?" he asked, his heart pounding in dread. He reached out, touched the back of her hand. "Are you all right?"

With a mournful moan, she shrank into herself.

Heedless of the rain that continued to fall, he put a hand to the wall and used his body to shield her from the curious eyes of those who passed. "Jessica?" He speared his fingers into her hair to lift it away from her face. "What happened?" When she continued to cry, he grasped her wrist. "Are you all right? Tell me what happened. Are you hurt?"

"I'm wet!" she cried from behind her hands.

He could see that, but there was still an icy cold image of something violent hovering in his mind. "Is that all? You weren't mugged or . . . anything?"

"I'm just wet! I got caught in the downpour, and there wasn't anywhere to go, and I wanted to look so nice. *I'm a mess*, Carter."

Carter was so relieved that she hadn't been bodily harmed in some other, darker, narrower alley, that he gave her a tight hug. "You're not a mess—"

"I'll get you wet," she protested, struggling to free herself from his hold.

He ignored her struggles. "You're looking goddamned sexy with that dress clinging to every blessed curve." When she gave a soft wail and went limp, he said, "Come on. Let's get you dry."

The next few minutes were a blur in Jessica's mind, principally because she didn't raise her eyes once. For the first time in her life, she was grateful that her hair was wild, because it fell by her cheeks like a veil. She didn't want Carter to see her, didn't want *anyone* to see her. She felt like a drowned rat, all the more pathetic in her own mind by contrast to the way she looked when she left Cambridge.

With a strong arm around her shoulder, Carter guided her out of the alley and into a cab. He didn't let her go even then, but spoke soft words to her during the short ride to his apartment. Wallowing in misery, she heard precious few of them. She kept her head down and her shoulders hunched. If she'd been able to slide under the seat, she'd have done just that.

He lived on Commonwealth Avenue, on the third floor of a time-honored six-story building. Naturally the rain had stopped by the time they reached it. He knew not to point that out to Jessica, and ushered her into the lobby before she could figure it out for herself. Though she'd stopped crying, she was distraught. The tension in her body wasn't to be believed.

"Here we go," he said as he quickly unlocked the door to his place. He led her directly into the bathroom, pulled a huge gray bath sheet from a shelf and began to wipe her arms. When he'd done what he could, he draped it around her, took a smaller towel, removed her glasses and dried them, too. "Better?"

Jessica refused to look at him. "I'm hopeless," she whispered.

"You're only wet," he said, setting the glasses by the sink. "When I saw you crying, leaning against the wall that way in the alley, I thought you'd been attacked. I honestly thought you'd been mugged. But you're only wet."

She was beyond being grateful for small favors. Turning her face away from him, she said in a woefully small voice, "I tried so hard. I wanted to look nice for you. I can't remember the last time anything meant so much to me, and I almost did it. I was looking good, and I was looking forward to tonight, and then it started to rain. I didn't know whether to go back or go on, and the rain came down harder, and then it didn't matter either way because I was soaked." Her eyes were filled with tears when they met Carter's. "It wasn't meant to be. I'm a disaster when it comes to nice things like dinner and the theater. There was a message in what happened."

"Like hell," Carter said, blotting her face with the smaller towel. "It rained. I would have been caught in it, too, if I'd walked, but I was running late, so I took a cab." He began to gently dry her hair. "Sudden storms come on like that. If it had come fifteen minutes earlier or later, you'd have been fine."

"But it didn't, and I'm not. And now everything is ruined. My dress, my shoes, my hair—"

"Your hair is gorgeous," he said, and it was. Moving the towel through it was like trying to tame a living thing. Waving naturally, it was wild and exotic. "You should wear it down like this more often. Then again, maybe you shouldn't. It's an incredible turn-on. Let everyone else see it tied up. Wear it down for me."

"There was a clip in it. It looked so pretty."

Carter found the clip buried in the maple-hued mass. "Here. Put it back in."

"I can't. I don't know how to do it. Mario did it."

"Mario?"

"My hairdresser."

She'd gone to the hairdresser. For a dinner and theater date with him. That fact, more than anything else she'd said, touched him deeply. He doubted she went to the hairdresser often, certainly not to have something as frivolous as a clip put in. But she'd wanted to look nice for him.

"Ah, Jessica." Towels and all, he took her in his arms. "I'm sorry you got rained on. You must have looked beautiful."

"Not beautiful. But nice."

"Beautiful."

"But I'm a mess. I can't go anywhere like this, not to dinner, not to the theater. Call someone else, Carter. Get someone else to go with you."

He held her back and stared down onto her face. "Are you kidding?"

"No. Call someone."

He was about to argue with her when he caught himself. "You're right," he said. "Stay put." He left the bathroom.

Sinking down onto the lip of the tub, Jessica hugged the towel around her. But it was no substitute for his arms. It had neither living warmth nor strength—either of which might have helped soothe the soul-deep ache of disappointment she felt.

She knew it shouldn't matter so much. What was one date? Or one dress? Or one hairdo? But she'd so wanted things to be right. She hadn't realized how *much* she'd wanted that. But it was all ruined. The dress, the hairdo, her evening with Carter.

"All set," he said, returning to the bathroom. He'd taken off his jacket and tie and was rolling up his sleeves.

"What are you doing?" she asked, staring at the finely corded forearms that were emerging.

"Getting you dry."

"But I thought you phoned—"

"The ticket agent. I did. He's calling the tickets in to the box office. They'll be resold in a minute. We've got new ones for next week. Friday night this time. Okay?"

"But I thought—"

Hunkering down before her, he said softly, "You thought I was calling someone else to go with me, when I've been telling you all along that I don't want to go with anyone else." Leaning forward, he gave her a light kiss. "You don't listen to me, Jessica."

"But I've ruined your evening."

"Not my evening. Our evening. And it's not ruined. Just changed."

"What can we possibly do?" she cried. Absurdly her eyes were tearing again. He was being so kind and good and understanding, and she hadn't been able to come through at all on her end. "I'm a mess!"

Carter grinned. It was a dangerously attractive grin. "Any more of a mess and I'd lay you right down on the floor and take you here. You really don't know how sexy you are, do you?"

"I'm not."

"You are." His grin faded as his eyes roamed her face. "You are, and I want you."

"Carter—"

"But that's not what we're going to do," he vowed as he rose to his full height. "We're going to dry you off and then go out for dinner."

She wanted that more than anything. "But I can't go anywhere! My dress is ruined!"

"Then we'll order in dinner and wait for your dress to dry. First, you'll have to take it off."

Her cheeks went pink. "I can't. I haven't anything to put on."

Raising a promising finger, he left her alone for as long as it took him to fetch a clean shirt from his closet. Back in the bathroom, he dropped it over the towel bar, stood her up, turned her and unwound the towel enough so that he could get at the back fastening of her dress.

"I can do that," she murmured, embarrassed.

"Indulge me." Gathering her hair to one side, he carefully released the hooks holding the turtleneck together. Her hair had protected that part of her dress from the rain, so the lime color there was more vivid. Carter wished he'd seen her before the storm, wished it with all his heart. He knew how sensitive Jessica was about her looks, but she'd felt good about herself then. He would have given anything to be able to share that good feeling with her.

Not that he didn't think she looked good now. He meant it when he said she looked sexy. He was aroused, and being so close to her, gently lowering her zipper, working it more slowly as the silk grew wetter wasn't doing anything to diminish that arousal. Nor was watching as each successive inch of ivory skin was exposed. He told himself to leave the bathroom, but the heat in his body was making his limbs lethargic. He knew he'd die if he couldn't touch that smooth soft skin just once.

His fingertips were light, tentative on her spine between the spot where her zipper ended and her bra began. He heard her catch her breath, but the sound was as feminine as the rest of her and couldn't possibly have stopped him. Leaving his thumb on her spine, he flattened his fingers, moved them back and forth over butter-softness, spread them until they disappeared under the drape of her dress.

"Carter?" she whispered.

He answered by bending forward and putting his mouth where his fingers had been. Eyes closed, he reveled in the sweet smell of her skin and the velvet smoothness beneath his lips. He kissed her at one spot, slid to the next and kissed her again.

Each kiss sent a charge of sexual energy flowing through her. She clutched the towel to her front, but it was a mindless kind of thing, a need to hold tight to something. Carter's touch sent her soaring. Her embarrassment at his helping her undress was taking a back seat to the pleasure of his caress, which went on and on. His mouth moved over her skin with slow allure, his breath warming what his tongue moistened, his hand following to soothe it all.

Her knees began to feel weak, but she wasn't the only one with the problem. Carter lowered himself to the edge of the laundry hamper. Drawing her between his thighs, he slid both hands inside her dress. His fingers spanned her waist, caressing her while his mouth moved higher. His hands followed, skipping over the slim band of her bra to her shoulders, gently nudging the silk folds of her dress forward.

Jessica tried again, though she was unable to produce more than a whisper. "Maybe this isn't such a good idea."

His breath came against the back of her neck, his voice as gritty as hers was soft. "It's the best one I've had. Tell me it doesn't feel good."

The days when she might have told him that, in pride and self-defense, were gone. "It feels good."

"Then let me do it. Just a little longer."

A small sigh slipped from her lips as she tipped her head to the side to make room for his mouth below her ear. What he was doing did feel good. His thighs flanked hers, offering support, and the whispering kisses he was pressing to her skin were seeping deep, soothing away the horror of the rain. The warmth of his hands, his mouth, his breath made her feel soft and cherished. Eyes closed, she savored the feeling as, minute by minute, she floated higher.

With the slightest pressure, Carter turned her to face him. Her eyes opened slowly to focus on his. She didn't need her glasses to see the heat that simmered amid the darkness there.

He touched her cheek with the side of his thumb, then slid his fingers to the back of her neck and brought her head forward. His mouth was waiting for hers, hot and hungry, and it wasn't alone in that. Jessica's met it with an eagerness that might have shocked her once, but seemed the most natural thing now. Because something had happened to her. She would never know whether it was the words of praise and reassurance he'd spoken, or the gentle, adoring way he touched and kissed her. But she was tired of fighting. She was tired of doubting, of taking everything he said and trying to analyze his motives. If she was being shortsighted, she didn't care. She wanted to feel and enjoy, and if there would be hell to pay in humiliation later, so be it. The risk was worth it. She wanted the pleasure now.

So she followed his lead, opening her mouth wider when he did, varying its pressure from heavy to feather light. There were times when their lips barely touched, when a kiss was little more than the exchange of breath or the touch of tongues, other times when the exchange was a more avid mating. She found one as exciting as the next, as stimulating in a breath-stopping, knee-shaking kind of way. When the knee-shaking worsened, she braced her forearms on his shoulders and anchored her fingers in his hair. She held him closer that way, wanted him closer still. And while the old Jessica was too much with her to say the words, the new Jessica spoke with the inviting arch of her body.

Carter heard her. His hands, which had been playing havoc over the gentle curves of her hips, came forward to frame her face. After giving her a final fierce kiss, he held her back.

For a time, he said nothing, just let himself drown with pleasure in the desire he saw in her eyes. If there'd ever been a different Jessica, he couldn't remember her. The only reality for him was the exquisitely sensual creature he now held between his legs.

Something else was between his legs, though, and it wasn't putting up with prolonged silence. Its heat and hardness were sending messages through the rest of his body that couldn't be ignored. His need to possess Jessica was greater than any need he'd ever known before.

His hands dropped from her face to her shoulders, then lower, to her breasts. He touched them gently, shaping his hand to their curve, brushing their hardened tips. Jessica gave a tiny sound of need and closed her eyes for a minute. When she opened them, Carter was smiling at her. "You're so beautiful," he murmured, and rewarded her for that with another kiss. This one was slower and more gentle, and by the time their lips parted, her breathing had quickened even more.

With her forearms on his shoulders and her forehead against his, she whispered, "I didn't know a kiss could do that."

"It's more than the kiss," Carter said in a low, slightly uneven voice. "It's my looking at you and touching you. And it's everything else that we haven't dared do. We've been thinking about it. At least, I have. I want to make love to you so badly, Jessica. Do you want that?"

It was a minute before she whispered, "Yes."

"Will you let me?"

"I'm frightened."

"You weren't frightened when I kissed you or when I touched your breasts."

"I was carried away."

His eyes met hers. "I'll carry you even further, if you let me. I want to do that. Will you let me?"

"I'm not good at lovemaking."

"Could've fooled me just now. I've never been kissed like that."

"You haven't?"

"You're a bombshell of innocence and raw desire. Do you have any idea how that combination turns a man on?"

She didn't, because she wasn't a man. But she knew that she was turned on herself. She could feel the pulsing deep inside her. "Will you tell me when I do things wrong?"

"You won't—"

"Will you tell me? I don't think I could bear it if we go through the whole thing and I think it's great, and then you tell me it wasn't so hot after all."

She'd spoken with neither accusation nor sarcasm, which was why Carter was so struck by what she said. After a moment of intense self-reproach, he murmured, "I wouldn't do that to you. I know you still don't trust me, but I swear, I wouldn't do that."

"Just tell me. If it's no good, we can stop."

He put a finger to her mouth. "I'll tell you. I promise. But that goes two ways. If I'm doing something you don't like, or something that hurts, I want you to tell me, too. Will you?" His finger brushed her lips, moving lightly, back and forth. "Will you?" he whispered.

She gave a small nod.

"Then come give me a kiss. One more kiss before we hang this dress up to dry."

8

JESSICA KISSED HIM with every bit of the love that had been building inside her for days. She hadn't put the correct name to it then, nor did she now, but that didn't matter. Under desire's banner, she gave her mouth to him in an offering that was as selfless as the deepest form of love. And when his kiss took her places she'd never been, she gave in to the luxury of it. And the newness. She'd never known such pleasure in a man's arms. She'd dreamed it, but to live the fantasy was something else.

Her headiness was such at the end of the kiss that she didn't demur when he drew her dress down. Leaving the damp silk gathered around her waist, he put his mouth to the soft skin that swelled above the cup of her bra. She held tight to his neck as he shifted his attention from one breast to the other, and what his mouth abandoned, his hand discovered. In no time, he had released the catch of her bra and was feasting on her bare flesh.

Jessica tried to swallow the small sounds of satisfaction that surged from inside.

"Say it," Carter urged against her heated flesh. "How does it feel?"

"Good," she gasped. She bent her head over his. "So good."

"I'm not doing it too hard?"

"Oh, no. Not too hard."

"Do you want it harder?"

"A little."

Her nipple disappeared into his mouth, drawn in by the force of his sucking, and she couldn't have swallowed her satisfaction this time if she'd tried. She choked out his name and buried her face in his hair. He was a beautiful man, making her feel beautiful. She was on top of the world.

The feeling stayed with her for a time. Gently, between long, deep kisses that set her heart to reeling, Carter eased the dress over her hips and legs. Then, keeping her mouth occupied without a break, he lifted her in his arms and carried her into the bedroom. His body followed hers down to the spread, hands gliding over her, learning the shape of her belly, her hips, her thighs. He couldn't quite believe she was there, couldn't seem to touch enough of her at once. And everywhere he touched, she responded with a sigh or a cry or the arch of her body, which excited him all the more. His breathing was ragged when he finally pulled away and began to tug at the buttons of his shirt.

Jessica missed the warmth of his touch at once. Opening her eyes to see where he'd gone, she watched him toss the shirt aside and undo his belt. Her insides were at fever pitch, needing him back with her, but her mind, in the short minute that he was gone, started to clear. She couldn't tear her eyes from him. With his hair ruffled and falling over his forehead, his chest bare and massive, and his clothes following one another to the carpet, he was more man than she had ever seen in her life.

She couldn't help but be frightened. She was too inexperienced, for one thing, to take watching him in stride. For another, she'd lived too long thinking of herself as a sexless creature to completely escape self-doubt. Inching up against the headboard, she drew in her legs and folded her arms over her breasts.

"Oh, no, you don't," Carter said, lunging after her. "No, you don't." The mattress bounced beneath his weight, but his fierceness gave way to a gentle grin as he took her wrists and flattened them on the pillow. "Please don't get cold feet on me now, honey. Not when we're so close, when I want you so badly."

"I—"

"No." His mouth covered hers, kissing her hungrily, but if he meant to drug her, he was the one who got high. His kiss gentled, grew lazier, and, in that, more seductive. With a low groan, he pulled her away from the headboard, up to her knees and against his body. She cried out when her breasts first touched his chest, but he held her there, stroking her back in such a way that not only her breasts, but her belly moved against him.

He groaned again. "That feels . . . so . . . nice."

She thought so, too. The hair on his chest was an abrasive against her sensitive breasts, chafing them in the most stimulating of ways. His stomach was lean, firm against her, and his arousal was marked, a little frightening but very exciting. Coiling her arms around his neck, she held on for dear life as the force of desire spiraled inside her.

"You were made for me," he whispered brokenly. "I swear you were made for me, Jessica. We fit together so well."

The words were nearly as pleasurable as the feel of his hard body against hers. His approval meant so much to her. She desperately wanted to please him.

"I'm not too thin?"

He ran a large hand over her bottom and hips. "Oh, no. You've got curves in all the right places."

"You didn't think so once."

"I was a jackass then. Besides, I didn't see you like this then." He dipped his fingers under the waistband of her panty hose, then withdrew them in the next breath and gently lay her back on the bed. His eyes were dark and avid as they studied her breasts, his hand worshiping as it cupped a rounded curve. Then he met her gaze. "I'm going to take off the rest. I want to see all of you."

She didn't speak over the thudding of her heart, but she gave a short nod. Though she'd never have believed it possible, she wanted him to see her. She wanted him to touch her. She wanted him to make love to her. She was living the fantasy, and in the fantasy, she was a beautiful, desirable woman. Her insides were a dark, aching vacuum needing to be filled in the way that only he could.

She lifted her hips to help him. Her panties slipped down her legs along with the nylons, and all the while she watched his eyes. They followed the stockings off, then retraced the route over her calves and thighs to the dark triangle at the notch of her thighs. There they lingered, growing darker and more smoky.

Lifting his gaze to hers, he whispered in awe, "You are so very, very lovely."

At that moment, she believed him, because that was part of the fantasy. She was trembling. Her bare breasts rose and fell with each shallow breath she took, and the knot of desire grew tighter between her legs. She wanted him to touch her, to ease the ache, but she couldn't get herself to say the words.

Carter didn't need them. He had never seen such raw desire in a woman's eyes, had never known how potent such a look could be. It was pushing him higher by the minute, making him shake beneath its force. His body clamored for release. He wasn't sure how much longer he could hold back. But he wanted it to be good, so good for her.

"So very lovely," he repeated in a throaty whisper. Tearing his eyes from hers, he lowered his gaze to her body. With an exquisitely light touch, he brushed the dark curls at the base of her belly. When she made a small sound, he looked back up in time to catch her closing her eyes, rolling her head to the side, pressing a fist to her mouth. He touched her again, more daringly this time. She made another small sound and, twisting her body in a subtly seductive way, arched up off the bed.

It was his turn to moan. He was stunned by the untutored sensuality he saw, couldn't quite believe that a woman with Jessica's potential for loving had lived such a chaste life. But she had. He had no doubts about it, particularly when she opened her eyes and seemed as stunned as he.

"How do you feel?" he whispered. He stroked her gently, delved more deeply into her folds with each stroke.

Raising her hands to the pillow, she curled them into fists and swallowed hard. "I need you," she whispered frantically. "Please."

Between the look in her eyes, the sound of her whisper and the intense arousal to which her straining body attested, Carter was pushed to the wall. His blood was rushing hotly through his veins. He knew he couldn't wait much longer to take the possession his throbbing body demanded.

He paused only to shuck his briefs, before coming over her. "Jessica?" Unfurling her fists, he wove his fingers through hers.

She tightened the grip. Her body rose to meet his. "Please, Carter."

Rational thought was becoming harder by the second. He fought to preserve those last threads. "Are you protected, honey? Are you using something?" When she gave a frustrated cry and lifted her head to open her mouth against his jaw, he whispered, "Help me. Tell me. Should I use something?"

"No," she cried, a tight, high-pitched wail. "I want a baby."

Swearing softly—and not trusting himself to stay where he was a minute longer, because the idea of her having his baby sent a shock wave of pleasure through him—he rolled off her and crossed the room to the dresser.

"Carter," she wailed.

"It's okay, honey. Hold on a second."

"I need you."

"I know. I'll be right there." A minute later, he was back, sitting on the edge of the bed to apply a condom. A minute after that, he was back over her, his hands covering hers, his mouth capturing hers. While he took her lips with a rabid hunger, he found his place between her thighs. Slowly and gently in contrast to his ravishment of her mouth, he entered her.

Her name was a low, growling sound surging from his throat, a sound of pleasure and relief when her tightness surrounded him. He squeezed his eyes shut in a battle against coming right then, but she wasn't helping his cause. She lifted her thighs higher around his in an instinctive move to deepen his penetration.

He looked down at her. Her face was flushed, lips moist and parted, eyes half-lidded and languorous. Her hair was wild, the dark waves fanning out over the slate-gray spread.

In an attempt to slow things down, he anchored her hips to the bed with the weight of his own and held himself still inside her. "Am I hurting you?" he whispered.

"Oh, no," she whispered back. "Does it feel okay?"

"More okay than it's ever felt," he answered. His words were hoarse, his breathing ragged. "You're so small and tight. Soft. Feminine. You have an incredible body. Incredible body. Are you sure I'm not hurting you?"

She managed a nod, then closed her eyes because even without his moving, the pressure inside her was building. "Please," she breathed.

"Please what?"

"Do something. I want . . . I need . . ."

He withdrew nearly all the way, returned to bury himself to the hilt. In reward for the movement, she cried out, then caught in the same breath and strained upward. "Carter!"

"That's it honey," he said, and began to move in earnest. "Do you feel me?"

"Yes."

"That what I want." Catching her mouth, he kissed her while the motion of his hips quickened. He pulled out and thrust in, filling her more and more, seeming to defy the laws of space. A fine sheen of sweat covered his body, blending with hers where their skin touched.

He had never known such pleasure, had never dreamed that such a physical act could touch his heart so deeply. But that was what was happening, and the heart touching was an aphrodisiac he couldn't fight. Long before he was ready to have the pleasure end, his body betrayed him by erupting into a long, powerful climax. Only when he was on the downside of that did he feel the spasms that were quaking inside Jessica.

Forcing his eyes open, he watched her face while the last of her orgasm shook her. With her head thrown back on the pillow, her eyes closed, her lips lightly parted, she was the most erotic being he'd ever seen in his life.

Her breathing was barely beginning to calm when his arms gave out. Collapsing over her, he lay with his head by hers for several minutes before rolling to the side and gathering her close. Then he watched her until she opened her eyes and looked up at him.

He smiled. "Hi."

"Hi," she said, shyly and still a bit breathlessly.

"You okay?"

She nodded, but when he expected her to look away, she didn't. Her eyes were increasingly large, expectant, trepidant.

"Having second thoughts?"

"One or two."

"Don't. Do you have any idea how good that was?" When she hesitated, then gave a short shake of her head against his arm, he brushed her eyebrow with a fingertip. "It was spectacular."

Still she hesitated. "Was it?"

"Yes." His smile faded. "You don't believe me."

She didn't say a thing for a minute, then spoke in a small voice, "I want to."

"But?"

She didn't answer at all this time, simply closed her eyes and lay her cheek on his chest. Carter would have prodded if he wasn't so enjoying lying quietly with her. But her body was warm, delicate, kittenish by his. Gently he drew her closer.

Her voice was flat, sudden in the silence. "Tom used to say things after it was over. He'd tell me how lacking I was."

Carter felt a chill, part anger, part disbelief, in the pit of his stomach. "Didn't he come?"

"Yes, but that didn't matter. He told me I wasn't much better than a sack of potatoes. I suppose I wasn't. I used to just lie there. I didn't want to touch him."

Carter remembered the way her hands had tightened around his, the way she'd arched to touch him with her body when he had restrained her hands, the way she brought her knees up to deepen his surge. She had been electric.

"That was Tom's fault," he said in a harsh voice. "It was his fault that he couldn't turn you on."

"I always felt inadequate."

"You shouldn't have. You're exquisite." Cupping her face in his hand, he kissed her lightly. "I have no complaints about what we did, except that I wanted it to last longer. But that was my fault. I couldn't hold back. I've been wanting you for days. I've been imagining incredible things, and to find out that the imagining wasn't half as incredible as the real thing—" He kissed her again, more deeply this time. His tongue lingered inside her mouth, withdrawing more slowly, reluctantly leaving her lips. "Jessica," he said in a shaky whisper and clutched her convulsively. But the feel of her body did nothing to dampen his reawakening desire.

Moaning, he released her and lay back on the bed.

Jessica came up on an elbow to eye him cautiously. "What's wrong?" she whispered.

He covered his eyes with his arm. "I want you again."

She looked at that arm, looked at the silky tufts of dark hair beneath it, looked at his chest, which was hairy in thatches, then his lean middle. By the time her eyes had lowered over his belly to the root of his passion, she was feeling tingly enough herself not to be as shocked by his erection as she might have been.

Without forethought, she touched his chest. He jumped, but when she started to snatch her hand away, he caught it, placed it back on his chest and laughed. "It's like lightning when you touch me. I wasn't prepared. That's all." Her hand was lying flat. "Go on. Touch. I like it."

Very slowly she inched her hand over the broad expanse of hair-spattered flesh and muscle. She felt those muscles tighten, felt his heartbeat accelerate, knew that her own was doing the same, but she wasn't about to stop. "I never dreamed..." Her fingertips lightly skimmed the dark, flat nipples that were already pebble hard.

"Never dreamed what?" he asked in a strained voice.

"That I'd...that we'd...you know."

"That we'd make love?"

"Mmm." Her thumb made a slow turn around his belly button.

Clapping a hand over hers, he pinned it to his stomach. When she looked up at him in surprise, his dark eyes smoldered. "Once before you touched me. Remember? By the duck pond?" She nodded. "I was wearing jeans then, and more than anything I wanted to unzip them and put your hand inside." He swallowed, then released her hand. "Touch me, Jessica?"

She looked from his eyes to his hardness and back.

"Touch me," he repeated in a beseechful whisper. The same beseechfulness was reflected in his eyes. More than anything else, that was what gave her courage.

Slowly her hand crept the short distance down a narrow line of hair to its flaring, finally to the part of him that stood, waiting straight and tall. She touched a tentative finger to him, surprised by the heat and the silkiness she found. Gradually her other fingers followed suit.

Taking in a ragged breath, Carter pushed himself into her hand. He wanted to watch her, wanted to see the expression on her face while she stroked him, but the agony of her touch was too much. She seemed to know just what to do and how fast. Closing his eyes, he savored her ministrations as long as he could before reaching down and tugging her back up. Then, when his mouth seized hers, his hands went to work.

He touched her everywhere, taking the time to explore that which he hadn't been able to do before. Where his hands left, his mouth took over. It wasn't long before Jessica was out of her mind with need, before he was, too.

Incredibly they soared higher this time. When it was done, their bodies were slick with sweat, their hearts were hammering mercilessly, their limbs were drained of energy.

They dozed off, awakening a short time later to find the sun down and the room dark. Carter left her side only long enough to light a low lamp on the dresser and draw the bedspread back. Then he took her with him between the sheets, settled her against him and faced the fact that he wanted her there forever.

"I love you," he whispered against her forehead.

Her eyes shot to his, held them for a minute before lowering. "No." She couldn't take the fantasy that far. "You're not thinking straight."

"I am. I've never said those words to a woman. I've never felt this way, felt this need to hold and protect and be with all the time. I've never wanted to wake up next to a woman, but I want it now. I don't like the idea of your going back home."

"I have to. It's where I belong"

His arm tightened. "You belong with me." When she remained silent, he said, "Do you believe in fate?"

"Predestination?"

"Mmm."

She didn't have to think about it long. "No. I believe that we get what we do. God helps those who help themselves."

But Carter disagreed. "If that were true, I'd never have returned home from Vietnam."

His words hovered in the air while Jessica's heart skipped a beat. Sliding her head back on his arm, she looked up at him. He was regarding her warily. "What do you mean?"

"I deserved to die. I hadn't done a decent thing in my life. I deserved to die."

"No one deserves to die in war."

"But someone always does." He looked away. "Good men died there. I saw them, Jessica. I saw them take hits. Some died fast, some slow, and with each one who went, I felt more like a snake."

"But you were fighting right alongside them," she argued.

"Yes, but they were good men. They were intelligent guys, guys with degrees and families and futures. A lot of them were rich—maybe not rich, but comfortable, and here I was walking around with a chip on my shoulder because I didn't have what they did. So they died, and I lived." He made a harsh sound, half laugh, half grunt. "Which says something, I guess, about the important things in life."

Jessica was beginning to understand. "That was what turned you around."

"Yes." His eyes held the fire of vehemence when they met hers. "Someone was watching over me there. Someone didn't let me die. Someone was telling me that I had things to do in life. I knew other guys who survived, but me, I never got the smallest scratch. That was fate. So was your asking me to work on Crosslyn Rise."

"Not fate. Gordon."

"But the setting was ripe for it." He turned on his side to look her in the eye. "Don't you see? You weren't married. You had been, but you were divorced. I never married. Never even had the inclination until I met you. Never wanted to think of having babies until I met you." Hearing the catch of her breath, he lowered his voice. "You do want them."

Her cheeks went red at the memory of what she'd cried out in the heat of passion.

He stroked that flush with his thumb. "I'll give you babies, Jessica. I couldn't take the chance before, because I wasn't sure you meant it. But you do, don't you?"

Silently she nodded.

"And until now the chances of it seemed remote, so you pushed it to the back of your mind. Then I said something about having children to leave the Rise to—"

"I won't be able to do that anyway. The Rise as I knew it will be gone."

"As you knew it. But all that's good about the Rise—its beauty and dignity, strength and stability—is inside you. You'll give that to your children. You'll make a wonderful mother."

Tears came to her eyes. What he was saying was too good to be true. *He* was too good to be true.

It was the aftermath of lovemaking, she decided. She didn't believe for a minute that he'd really want to marry her. Give him a day or two and he'd realize how foolish his talk was.

"I love you," he whispered, and she didn't argue. He kissed her once, then a second time, but the stirring he felt wasn't so much in his groin as in the region of his heart. He wanted to take care of her, to give her things, to do for her. She was a gentle woman, a woman to be loved and protected. He would do that if she let him.

Rubbing her love-swollen lips with the tip of his finger, he said, "You must be hungry."

"A little."

"If I order up pizza, will you have some?"

"Sure."

He kissed her a final time, then rolled away from her and out of bed. She watched him cross the room to the closet. His hips were narrow, his buttocks tight, the backs of his thighs lean and muscled, and if she'd thought that his walk was seductive when he was dressed, naked it was something else. When he put on a short terry-cloth robe, the memory of his nudity remained. When he returned to her, carrying the shirt from the bathroom, she felt shy.

"Uh-uh," he chided when she averted her eyes. "None of that." He helped her on with the shirt. "I've seen everything. I *love* everything."

"I'm not used to this, I guess," she murmured, fumbling with the buttons.

He could buy that, and in truth, he liked her shyness. It made the emergence of her innate sensuality that much more of a gift. "I'll give you time," he said softly, and led her out of the bedroom.

He was going to have to give her plenty of that, she mused a short time later. They sat on stools at the kitchen counter, eating the pizza that had just been delivered. Though it was a mundane act, she'd never done anything so cataclysmic. She couldn't believe that she was sitting there with Carter Malloy, that she was wearing nothing under his shirt, that she'd worn even less not long before.

Carter Malloy. It boggled her mind. *Carter Malloy.*

"What is it?" he asked with a perplexed half smile.

She blushed. "Nothing."

"Tell me."

Tipping her head to the side, she studied a piece of pizza crust. "I'm very... surprised that I'm here."

"You shouldn't be. We've been building toward this for a while."

He was right, but she wasn't thinking of the recent past. "I'm thinking farther back. I really hated you when I was little." She dared him a look and was struck at once by his handsomeness. "You're so different. You look so different. You *act* so different. It's hard to believe that a person can change so much."

"We all have to grow up."

"Some people don't. Some people just get bigger. You've really changed." Studying him, she was lured on by the openness of his features. "What about before Vietnam? I can understand how your experience there could shape your future, but what about your past? Why were you the way you were? It couldn't have been the money factor alone. What was it all about?"

Thoughtfully pursing his lips, Carter looked down at his hands. His mouth relaxed, but he didn't look up. "The money thing was a scapegoat. It was a convenient one, maybe even a valid one on some levels. Since my parents worked at Crosslyn Rise, we lived in town, and that town happens to be one of the wealthiest in the state. So I went to school with kids who had ten times more than me. From the very start, I was different. They all knew each other from kindergarten. I was a social outcast from the beginning, and it was a self-perpetuating thing. I was never easy to get along with."

"But why? If you were still that way, I'd say that it was a genetic thing that you couldn't control. But you're easy enough to get along with now, and you don't seem to be suffering doing it. So if it wasn't genetic, it had to come from outside you. Some of it may have come from antagonism in school, but if you were that way when you first enrolled, it had to come from your family. That's what I don't understand. Annie and Michael were always wonderful, easygoing people."

"You weren't their son," Carter said with a sharpness reminiscent of a similar comment he'd made once before.

Not for a minute did Jessica feel that the sharpness was directed at her. He was thinking back to his childhood. She could see the discomfort in his eyes. "What was it like?" she asked, needing to understand him as intimately as possible.

"Stifling."

"With Annie and Michael?" she asked in disbelief.

"They loved me to bits," he explained. "I was their pride and joy, their hope for the future. I was going to be everything they weren't, and from the earliest they told me so. I'm not sure that I understood what it all meant at the time, but when I was slow doing things, they pushed me. I didn't like being pushed—I still don't, so maybe that's a biological trait after all. I stayed in the terrible-two stage for lots of years, and by that time, a pattern had been set. My parents were always on top of me, so I did whatever I could to thwart them. I think I was hoping that at some point they'd just give up on me."

"But they never did."

"No," he said quietly. "They never did. They were always loyal and supportive." He looked at her then. "Do you know how much pressure that can put on a person?"

Jessica was beginning to see it. "They kept hoping for the best and you kept disappointing them."

"By the time I was a teenager, I had a reputation of being tough. That hurt my parents, too. People would look at them with pity, wondering how they ever managed to have a son like me."

She remembered thinking the same thing herself, and not too long before. "They are such quiet, gentle people."

Again Carter looked away, pursing his lips. He felt guilty criticizing his parents, yet he wanted Jessica to know the truth, at least as he saw it. "Too quiet and gentle. Especially my dad."

"You would have liked him to be stronger with you?"

"With me, with *anyone*. He wasn't strong, period."

It occurred to Jessica that she'd never thought one way or another about Michael Malloy's strength. "In what sense?"

"As a man. My mother ran the house. She did everything. I can't remember a time when Dad doted on her, when he stood up for her, when he bought her a gift. The only thing he ever did was the gardening."

"Do you think she resented that?"

"Not really. I think it suited her purposes. She liked being the one in control." He took a minute to consider what he'd said. "So maybe when I use the word 'stifling' I should be using the word 'controlling.' In her own quiet way, my mother was the most controlling woman I've ever met. That was what I spent my childhood rebelling against—that, and the fact that my father never once opened his mouth to complain when, in her own gentle way, she ran roughshod over him."

He grew quiet, then looked down. "Lousy of me to be bad-mouthing them, when I treated them so poorly, huh?"

"You're not bad-mouthing them. You're just explaining what you felt when you were growing up."

He met her gaze. "Does it make any sense?"

"I think so. I always thought of Annie as, yes, gentle and quiet, but also efficient. Very efficient. She definitely took control of things in our house. I can understand how 'taking control' could become 'controlling' in her own house. And Michael was always gentle and quiet...just...gentle and quiet. That was what I liked about him. He was always pleasant, always smiled. For me, that was a treat."

"It used to drive me wild. I'd do anything just to rile him."

"Did you manage?"

Carter smirked. "Not often. And he's still like that. Still quiet and gentle. I doubt he'll ever change."

Jessica was relieved to hear the fondness in his voice. "You've accepted him, then?"

"Of course. He's my father."

"And you're close to him now?"

"Close? I don't know, close. We talk regularly on the phone, but for every five minutes Dad's on, Mom's on for ten. I suppose it's just as well. They like to hear what I'm doing, but I'm not sure they appreciate the details." He gave an ironic smile. "I've finally made it, just like they wanted me to, but that means my world is very different from theirs."

"Are they happy?"

"In Florida? Yes."

"For you?"

"Very." His smile was sheepish this time. "Of course, they don't know why I have a partner, since I can do so much better by myself. And they don't know why I'm not married."

Jessica knew they'd be pleased if Carter ever told them he loved her, but she prayed he wouldn't do that. To tie their hopes to something that would never go anywhere was a waste. Even if Carter did believe that he loved her, he'd see the truth once he got back to his normal, everyday life. The fewer people who knew of the night he'd spent playing at being in love, the better.

JESSICA RETURNED to Crosslyn Rise on Friday, soon after Carter left for work. She wanted to immerse herself in her own world, to push the events of Thursday night to the back of her mind.

That was easier said than done, because after dinner, they'd gone back to bed. Time and again during the night, they'd made love, and while Jessica never once initiated the passion, she took an increasingly aggressive part in it. That gave her more to think about than ever.

She seemed to bloom in Carter's arms. Looking back on some of the things she'd done, she shocked herself. She, who had never hungered for another man, had lusted for his body, and she couldn't even say that he taught her what to do. Impulses had just...come. She had wanted to touch him, so she had. She had wanted to taste him, so she had.

And he hadn't complained. Every so often, when she'd caught herself doing something daring, she'd paused, but in each case he had urged her on. In each case his pleasure had been obvious, which made her feel all the freer.

Freer. Free. Yes, she had felt that, and it was the strangest thing of all. Making love to Carter, even well after that first pent-up desire had been slaked, was a relief. With each successive peak she reached, she felt more relaxed. It was almost as if she'd done just what he had once accused her of doing—spent years and years denying her instincts, so that now she felt the sheer joy of letting them out.

She fought the idea of that. Once discovered, the passion in her wouldn't be as easily tucked away again— which was just fine, as long as Carter stayed with her. But she couldn't count on that happening. In the broad light of a Crosslyn Rise day, she had too many strikes against her.

She was plain. She was boring. She was broke.

Carter was just the opposite. He was on his way up in the world, and he would make it. She knew that now. She also knew that he didn't need someone like her weighing him down.

That was one of the reasons why, when he called at four to say that he was leaving the office and would be at Crosslyn Rise within the hour, she told him not to come.

9

"WHY NOT?" Carter asked, concerned. "Is something wrong?"

"I just think that I ought to get some work done."

"You've had all day to do that."

"Well, I slept for some of the day, and I didn't concentrate well for the rest."

He didn't have to ask why on either score. "So give it up for today. You won't get much done anyway."

"I'd like to try."

"Try tomorrow. We agreed on dinner tonight."

"I know, but I'm not very hungry."

"Not now. But it'll be an hour before I get there, another hour before we get to a restaurant and get served." He paused, then scolded, "You're avoiding the issue. Come on, Jessica. Spit it out."

"There's nothing to spit out. I'd just rather stay home tonight."

"Okay. We'll stay home."

He was being difficult, she knew, and that frustrated her. "I'd rather be alone."

"You would not. You're just scared because everything that happened last night was sudden and strong."

"I'm not scared," she protested. "But I need time, Carter."

"Like hell you do," he replied, and slammed down the phone.

FORTY MINUTES LATER, he careened up the driveway and slammed on his brakes. He was out of the car in a flash, taking the steps two at a time, and he might well have pounded the door down had not Jessica been right there to haul it open after his first fierce knock.

"You have no right to race out here this way," she cried, taking the offensive before he could. She was wearing a shirt and jeans, looking as plain as she could, and as angry. "This is my house, my life. If I say that I want to spend my evening alone, that's what I want to do!"

Hands cocked low on his hips, Carter held his ground. "Why? Give me one good reason why you want to be alone."

"I don't have to give you a reason. All I have to say is yes or no."

"This morning you said yes. What happened between now and then to make you change your mind?"

"Nothing."

"What happened, Jessica?"

"Nothing!"

His brown eyes narrowed. "You started thinking, didn't you? You started thinking about all the reasons why I can't possibly feel the way I say I do about you. You came back to this place, and suddenly last night was an aberration. A fluke. A lie. Well, it wasn't, Jessica. It isn't. I loved you then, and I love you now, and you can say whatever stupid things you want, but you can't change my mind."

"Then you're the fool, because I don't want to get involved."

"Baloney." His eyes bore into hers, alive with a fire that was only barely tempered in his voice. "You want a husband, and you want kids. You can pretend that you don't, and maybe it used to work, but it won't work now. Because, whether you like it or not, you *are* involved. You can't forget what happened last night."

"What an arrogant thing to say!"

"Not arrogant. Realistic, and mutual. I can't forget it, either. I want to do it again."

"You're a sex fiend."

His voice grew tighter, reflecting the strain on his patience. "Sex had nothing to do with what we did. That was lovemaking, Jessica. We *made* love, because we *are* in love. If you don't want to admit it, fine. I can wait. But I'm going to say it whenever I want. I love you."

"You do not," she scoffed, and pushed up her glasses.

"I love you."

"You may think you do, but give yourself a little time, and you'll come to your senses. You don't love me. You can't possibly love me."

"Why not?" He took a step toward her, and his voice was as ominous as his look. "Because you're not pretty? Because you lie like a sack of potatoes in my bed? Because you're a bookworm?"

"It's Crosslyn Rise that you love."

He eyed her as though she were crazy. "Crosslyn Rise is some land and a house. It's not warm flesh and blood like me."

"But you love it, you associate me with it, hence you think you love me."

"Brilliant deduction, Professor, but wrong. You're losing Crosslyn Rise. There's no reason why I would align myself with you if the Rise is what I want."

She took a different tack. "Then it's the money. If this project goes through, you'll be making some money. So you're confusing the issues. You feel good about the money, so you feel good about me."

"I don't want the money that bad," he said with a curt laugh. "If you were a loser, no amount of money would lure me into your bed."

"What a crass thing to say!"

"It's the truth. And it should say something about my feelings for you. We did it last night more times than I've ever done it in a single night before. My muscles are killing me. Still I want more. Every time I think of you I get hard."

She pressed her hands to her ears, because his words alone could excite her. Only when his mouth remained still did she lower her hands and say very slowly, "Revenge is a potent aphrodisiac."

"*Revenge.* What in the hell are you talking about?"

She tipped up her chin. "This is the ultimate revenge, isn't it? For all those years when I had everything you wanted?"

"Are you kidding?" he asked, and for the first time there was an element of pain in his voice. "Didn't you hear a word I said last night? Didn't any of it sink in—any of the stuff about Vietnam or my parents? I've never told anyone else about those things. Was it wasted on you?"

"Of course not."

"But I didn't get through. You wanted to know what caused me to change over the years, and I told you, but I didn't get through." He paused, and the pain was replaced by a sudden dawning. "Or was that what frightened you most, because for the first time you could believe that the change was for real?" He took a step closer. "Is that it? For the first time you had to admit that I might, just might be the kind of guy you'd want to spend the rest of your life with, and that scares you." He took another step forward. Jessica matched it with one back. "Huh?" he goaded. "Is that it?"

"No. I don't want to spend the rest of my life with *any* man."

"Because of your ex-husband? Because of what he did?"

She took another step back as he advanced. "Tom and I are divorced. What he did is over and done."

"It still haunts you."

"Not enough to shape my future." She kept moving back.

"But you don't trust me. That's the crux of the problem. You don't trust that I'm on the level and that I won't hurt you the way that selfish bastard did. Damn it, Jessica, how can I prove to you that I mean what I say if you won't see me?"

"I don't want you to prove anything," she said, but her heels had reached the first riser of the stairs. When he kept coming, she sat down on the steps.

"Okay." He put one hand flat on the tread by her hip. "I'll admit things have happened quickly. If you want time, I'll give you time. I won't rush you into anything, especially something as important as marriage." He put his other hand by her other hip. His voice lowered. His eyes dropped to her mouth. "But I won't stand off in the distance or out of sight, either. I can't do that. I need to see you. I need to be with you."

Jessica wanted to argue, but she was having trouble thinking with him so close. She could see the details of the five-o'clock shadow that he hadn't had time to shave, could feel the heat of his large body, could smell the musky scent that was his alone. He looked sincere. He sounded sincere. She wanted to believe him . . . so . . . badly.

His mouth touched hers, and she was lost. Memory of the night before returned in a storm of sensation so strong that she was swept up in it and whirled around. She had to wrap her arms around his waist to keep herself anchored to something real, and then it wasn't memory that entranced her, but the sensual devouring of his mouth.

Over and over he kissed her, dueling with her lips for supremacy in much the same way they'd argued, though neither seemed to care who won, and, in fact, both did. When her glasses fogged up, he took them off and set them aside. Pressing her back on the stairs, he touched her breasts, then slid his fingers between the buttons of her shirt to reach bareness. When that failed to satisfy his craving, he unbuttoned the shirt and unhooked her bra, but no sooner had he exposed her flesh than she brushed the back of her hand over the rigid display on the front of his slacks.

"Oh, baby," he said, "come here." Slipping a large hand under her bottom, he lowered himself and pressed her close. In the next breath, he was kissing her again, and in the next, tugging at the fastening of her jeans.

"Carter," she whispered, breathless. "What—"

"I need you," he gasped, pushing at her zipper.

"Now?"

"Oh, yeah."

"Here?"

"Anywhere. Help me, Jess." He'd turned his attention to his belt, which was giving him trouble. Jessica did what she could, but her hands were shaky and kept tangling with his, and when it came to his zipper, his erection made things even more difficult. After a futile pass or two, the most important thing seemed to be freeing her own legs from their bonds.

She didn't quite make it. Her jeans were barely below her knees when Carter pressed her back to the steps. With a single strong stroke, he was inside her, welcomed there hotly and moistly. Then the movement of his hips drove her wild, and she didn't care that they were in the front hall, that they were half-dressed, that the ghosts of Crosslyn Rise were watching, turning pink through their pallor. All she cared about was sharing a precious oneness with Carter.

THAT WEEKEND WAS THE HAPPIEST Jessica had ever spent, because Carter didn't leave her for long. He made love to her freely, wherever and whenever the mood hit. And wherever or whenever that was, she was ready. Hard as it was to believe, the more they made love, the more she wanted him.

As long as he was with her, she was fine. As long as he was with her, she believed his words of love, believed that his ardor could be sustained over the years and years he claimed, believed that his head would never be turned by another woman.

When he left her on Monday morning to go to work, though, she thought of him at the office, in restaurants, with clients, and she worried. She went to work, herself, and she was the quiet, studious woman she'd always been.

Maybe if people had looked at her strangely she would have felt somehow different. But she received the same smiles and nods from colleagues she passed. No one looked twice, as had happened when she'd dressed up the Thursday before. No one seemed remotely aware of the kind of weekend she'd spent.

She didn't know what she expected. Aside from a bundle of tender muscles, she was no different physically than she'd always been. But no one knew about the muscles. No one knew about Carter Malloy. No one knew about the library sofa, the parlor rug or the attic cot.

So she saw herself as the others saw her, and everything that was risky and frightening about her affair with Carter was magnified.

Until she saw him that night. Then the doubts seemed to waft into the background and pop like nothing more weighty than a soap bubble, and she came to life in his arms.

The pattern repeated itself over the next few weeks. Her days were filled with doubts, her nights with delight. Graduation came and went, and the summer session began, but for the first time in her life, there was a finite end to a day's work. That end came when Carter arrived. He teased her about it, even urged her to do some reading or class preparation on those occasions when he had brought work of his own with him to do, but she couldn't concentrate when he was with her. She would sit with a book while he worked, but her eyes barely touched the page, and her mind took in nothing at all but how he looked, what he was doing, what they'd done together minutes, hours or days before.

She was in love. She admitted it, though not to him. Somehow, saying the words was the most intense form of self-exposure, and though one part of her wished she had the courage because she knew how much he wanted to hear it, she wasn't that brave. She felt as though she were driving on a narrow mountain path where one moment's inattention could tip her over the edge. She wanted to be prepared when Carter's interest waned. She wanted to have a remnant of pride left to salvage.

HIS INTEREST WANED neither in her nor in Crosslyn Rise. Sketch after sketch he made, some differing from the others in only the most minor of features, but he wanted them to be right. He and Jessica had dinner one night with Nina Stone to get her opinion on the needs of the local real estate market; as a result of that meeting, they decided to offer six different floor plans, two each in two-bedroom, three-bedroom and four-bedroom configurations.

Also as a result of that meeting, Jessica learned that Carter wasn't interested in Nina Stone. Nina was interested in him; her eyes rarely left his handsome face, and when she accompanied Jessica to the ladies' room, she made her feelings clear.

"He's quite a piece of man. If things cool between you two, will you tell me?"

Jessica was surprised that Nina had guessed there was something beyond a working relationship between her and Carter. "How did you know?" she asked, not quite daring to look Nina in the eye.

"The vibes between you. They're hot. Besides, I've been sending him every come-hither look I know, and he hasn't caught a one. Honey, he's smitten."

"Nah," Jessica said, pleased in spite of herself. "We're just getting to know each other again." Far better, she knew, to minimize things, so that it wouldn't be as humiliating if the relationship ended.

Still there was no sign of that happening. On the few occasions that Carter mentioned Nina after their meeting, it was with regard to the project and with no more than a professional interest.

"Didn't you think she was pretty?" Jessica finally asked.

"Nina?" He shrugged. "She's pretty. Not soft and gentle like you, though, or half as interesting."

As though to prove his point, he spent hours talking with her. They discussed the economy, the politics in Jessica's department, the merits of a book that he'd read and had her read. He was genuinely curious about what she was thinking, was often relieved to find that she wasn't lost on some esoteric wavelength where he couldn't possibly join her.

When it came to Crosslyn Rise, he took few steps without having her by his side, considered few ideas without trying them out on her first. Though her feedback wasn't professional from an architectural standpoint, it was down-to-earth. When she didn't like something, she usually had good reason. He listened to her, and while he didn't always agree, he yielded as many times as not. Their personal, vested interests balanced each other out; when he was too involved in the design to think of practicality, she reminded him of it, and when she was too involved in the spirit of Crosslyn Rise to see the necessity of a particular architectural feature, he pointed it out.

By the middle of July, there was a set of plans to show Gordon. As enthusiastic about them as Carter was, Jessica set up the meeting. Then the two of them stood side by side, closely watching for Gordon's reaction as he looked over the drawings.

He liked them, though after he'd said, "You two make a good team," for the third time in ten minutes, Jessica was wondering what particular message he was trying to get across. She had tried not to look at Carter, and when he caught her hand behind her skirt and drew it to the small of his back, she was sure Gordon couldn't see.

Possibly he had sensed the same vibes Nina had, though she hadn't thought Gordon the type to sense vibes, at least not of that kind. She finally decided that it was the little things that gave them away—the light lingering of Carter's hand on her back when they first arrived, the way he attributed her ideas to her rather than taking credit for them himself, the mere fact that they weren't fighting.

The last made the most sense of all. Jessica remembered her reaction when Gordon had first mentioned Carter's name. She thought back to that day, to her horror and the hurt in those memories. At some point along

the way, the hurt had faded, she realized. She had super-
imposed fondness and understanding on the Carter Malloy who had been so angry with the world and himself,
and doing that took the sting off the things he'd once said.
Not that she dwelt on those memories. He had given her
new ones, ones that were lovely from start to finish.

"Jess?" Carter's low, gentle voice came through her
reverie. She looked up in surprise, smiled a little shame-
facedly when she realized her distraction. He motioned to
the nearby chair. Blushing, she sank into it.

"Everything all right, Jessica?" Gordon asked.

"Fine. Just fine."

"You know these highbrow types," Carter teased, smiling indulgently. "Always dreaming about one thing or
another."

Her cheeks went even redder, but she latched onto the
excuse as a convenient out. "Did I miss anything?"

"Only Gordon's approval. I have to polish up the
drawings some, but he agrees that we're ready to move
ahead."

Jessica's eyes flew to Gordon. "Getting the investors together?"

Gordon nodded and opened a folder that had been lying
on the corner of his desk. He removed two stapled parcels, handed one to each of them, then took up his own.
"I've jumped the gun, I guess, but I figured that I'd be doing
this work anyway, so it wouldn't matter. These are the
names and profiles of possible investors, along with a list
of their general assets and the approximate contribution
they might be counted on to make. You can skip through
page one—that's you, Jessica—and page two—that's you,
Carter. The next three are William Nolan, Benjamin
Heavey and Zachary Gould. You know Ben, don't you,
Carter?"

"Sure do. I worked with him two years ago on a development in North Andover." To Jessica, he said, "He's been involved in real estate development for fifteen years. A conservative guy, but straight. He's selective with his investments, but once he's in, he's in." He looked at Gordon. "Is he interested?"

"When I mentioned your name, he was. I didn't want to tell him much else until the plans were finalized, but he just cashed in on a small shopping mall in Lynn, so he has funds available. Same with Nolan and Gould."

Jessica was trying to read as quickly as possible, but she'd barely made it halfway down the first sheet on Benjamin Heavey when Gordon mentioned the others. "Nolan and Gould?" She had to flip back a page to reach Nolan, ahead two to reach Gould.

"Are you familiar with either name?" Gordon asked.

"Not particularly." Guardedly she looked up. "Should I be?"

Carter shot her a dry grin. "Only if you're into reading the business section of the paper," which he knew, for a fact, she was not, since they'd joked about it just the Sunday before, when she'd foisted that particular section on him in exchange for the editorials.

"Bill Nolan is from the Nolan Paper Mill family," Gordon explained. "He started in northern Maine, but has been working his way steadily southward. Even with the mills up north, he has a genuine respect for the land. A project like this would be right up his alley."

Carter agreed. "From what I hear, he's not out for a killing, which is good, since he won't get one here. What he'll get is a solid return on his investment. He'll be happy." Turning several pages in his lap, he said to Gordon, "Tell me about Gould. The name rings a bell, but I can't place it."

"Zach Gould is a competitor of mine."

"A banker?" Jessica asked.

"Retired, actually, though he's not yet sixty. He was the founder and president of Pilgrim Trust and its subsidiaries. Two years ago he had a heart attack, and since he was financially set, he took his doctor's advice and removed himself from the fray. So he dabbles in this and that. He's the type who would drop in at the site every morning to keep tabs on the progress. Nice guy. Lonely. His wife left him a few years back, and his children are grown. He'd like something like this."

Jessica nodded. Determined to read the fine print when she had time alone later, she turned to the next page. "John Sawyer?"

Gordon cleared his throat. "Now we start on what I like to call the adventurers. There are three of them. None can contribute as much money as any of these other three men, or you or Carter, but each has good reason not only to want to be involved but to be sure that the project is a success." He paused for only as long as it took Carter to flip to the right page. "John Sawyer lives here in town. He owns the small bookstore on Shore Drive. I'm sure you've been there, Jessica. It's called The Leaf Turner?"

She smiled. "Uh-huh. It's a charming place, small but quaint." Her smile wavered. "I don't remember seeing a man there, though. Whenever I've been in, Minna Larken has helped me."

Gordon nodded. "You've probably been in during the morning or early afternoon hours. That's when John is home taking care of his son. By the time two-thirty rolls around, he has high school girls come in to play with the boy while he goes to work."

"How old is the kid?" Carter asked.

"Three. He'll be entering school next year. Hopefully."

At the cautious way he'd added the last, Jessica grew cautious herself. "Something's wrong with him?"

"He has problems with his hearing and his eyesight. John had tried him in a preschool program, but he needs special attention. He'll have a tough time in the public kindergarten class. There is a school that would be perfect for him, but it's very expensive."

"So he could use a good money-making venture," Carter concluded. "But does he have funds for an initial investment?"

Gordon nodded. "His wife died soon after the boy was born. There was some money in life insurance. John was planning to leave it in the bank for the child's college education, but from the looks of things he won't get to college unless he gets special help sooner."

"How awful," Jessica whispered, looking helplessly from Gordon to Carter and back. "She must have been very young. How did she die?"

"I don't know. John doesn't talk about it. They were living in the Midwest when it happened. He moved here soon after. He's a quiet fellow, very bright but private. In many respects, the stakes are higher for John than for some of these others. But he's been asking me about investments, and this is the most promising to come along in months."

"But will the money come through in time for him?" Carter asked. "If all goes well, we could break ground this fall and do a fair amount of framing before winter sets in. We may be lucky enough to make some preconstruction sales, but most of the units won't be ready for aggressive marketing until next spring or summer, and then the bank loans will have to be paid off first. I can't imagine that any of us will see any raw cash for eighteen months to two years. So if he's going to need the money sooner—"

"I think he's covered for the first year or two. But when he realized that the child's education was going to be a long-time drain, he knew he had to do something else."

"By all means," Jessica said, "ask him to join us." She focused her attention on the next sheet. "Gideon Lowe." She glanced at Carter. "Didn't you mention him to me once?"

"To you and to Gordon. You did call him then?" he asked the banker.

"By way of a general inquiry, yes. I named you as the contact. He thinks you're a very talented fellow."

"I think he's even more so. He takes pride in his work, which is more than I can say for some builders I know. Now that they're getting ridiculous fees for the simplest jobs, they've become arrogant. And lazy. Cold weather? Forget it—they can't work in cold weather. Rain? Same thing. And if the sun is out, they want to quit at twelve to play golf."

"I take it Gideon Lowe doesn't play golf?" Jessica asked.

"Not quite," Carter confirmed with a knowing grin. "Gideon would die strolling around a golf course. He's an energetic man. He needs something fast."

"Like squash?" she asked, because squash was Carter's game, precisely for its speed, as he'd pointed out to her in no uncertain terms.

"Like basketball. He was All-American in high school and would have gone to college on a basketball scholarship if he hadn't had to work to support his family."

Jessica's eyes widened. "Wife and kids?"

"Mother and sisters. His mother is gone now, and his sisters are pretty well-set, but he's too old to play college basketball. So he plays on a weekend league. Summers, he plays evenings." Recalling the few games he'd watched,

Carter gave a slow head shake. "He's got incredible moves, for a big guy."

"And incredible enthusiasm," Gordon interjected. "He made me promise to call him as soon as I had something more to say about Crosslyn Rise."

"Then you should call him tomorrow," Jessica said, because Carter's recommendation was enough for her. She turned to the final page on her lap and her eyes widened. "Nina Stone?" She looked questioning at Gordon.

"Miss Stone called me," Gordon explained with a slight emphasis on the me. "She knows something of what you're doing since you've talked with her. She knows that I'm putting a group together. She wants to be included in that group and she has the money to do it."

Jessica sent him an apologetic look. "She was insistent?"

"You could say that."

"It's her way, Gordon. Some people see it as confidence, and it sells lots of houses. I can imagine, though, that it would be a little off-putting with someone like you, particularly on the phone. Wait until you meet her, though. She's a bundle of energy." As she said it, she had an idea. Turning to Carter, she said, "I'll bet she and Gideon would get along. You didn't say if he was married."

"He's not, but forget it. They are two very forceful personalities. They'd be at each other's throats in no time. Besides," he added, and a naughty gleam came into his eye, "they're all wrong physically. She's too little and he's too big. They'd have trouble making . . . it, uh, you know what I mean."

She knew exactly what he meant, but she wasn't about to elaborate in front of Gordon any more than he was. The only solace for her flaming cheeks was the rush of color to Carter's.

Fortunately, that color didn't hinder his thinking process. Recovering smoothly, he said, "If Nina has the money, I see no reason why she shouldn't invest." More serious, he turned to Jessica. "What's her motive?"

"She wants to go into business for herself. She wants the security of knowing she's her own boss. How about Gideon?"

"He wants the world to know he's his own boss. Respect is what he's after."

"Doesn't he have it now?"

"As a builder, yes. As a man who works with his hands, yes. As a man with brains as well as brawn, no. He's definitely got the brains—that's what makes him so successful as a builder. But people don't always see it that way. So he wants to be involved with the tie-and-jacket crowd this time."

Jessica could understand how Carter might understand Gideon better than some. He'd seen both sides. "If Gideon wants to invest, would that rule out his doing the building?"

"I hope not," Carter said, and looked questioningly at Gordon.

"I don't see why it would," Gordon answered. "The body of investors will be bound together by a legal agreement. If Gideon should decide to bid on the job and then lose out to another builder, his position in the consortium will remain exactly the same."

"There wouldn't be a conflict of interest?"

"Not at all. This is a private enterprise." He arched a brow toward Jessica. "Theoretically, you could pick your builder now, and make it part of the package."

"I wouldn't know who to pick," she said on impulse, then realized that she was supposed to be in charge. Recomposing herself, she said to Gordon, "You pointed out that I have to be willing to listen to people, especially when they know more about things than I do. I think that Carter will help me decide on the builder. Do you have any problem with that?"

"Me? None. None at all."

Something about the way he said it gave Jessica pause. "Are you sure?"

Gordon frowned at the papers before him for a minute before meeting her gaze. "I may be out of line saying this—" his gaze broke off from hers for a minute to touch on Carter before returning "—but I didn't expect that you two would be so close."

"We're very close," Carter said, straightening slightly in his seat. "With a little luck we'll be married before long."

"Carter!" Jessica cried, then turned to Gordon, "Forget he said that. He gets carried away sometimes. You know how it is with men in the spring."

"It's summer," Carter reminded her, "and the only thing that's relevant about that is that you'll have a few weeks off between semesters at the end of August when we could take a honeymoon."

"Carter!" She was embarrassed. "Please, Gordon. Ignore this man."

To her chagrin, Gordon looked to be enjoying the banter. "I may be able to, but the reason I raise the issue is that other people won't." He grew more sober. "It was clear from the minute you two walked in here that something was going on. I think you ought to know just what that something is before you face the rest of this group. The last thing you want them to feel is that they're at the end of a rope, swinging forward and back as your relationship does."

"They won't," Jessica said firmly.

"Are you sure?"

"Very. This is a business matter. Whatever my relationship is or isn't with Carter, I'll be very professional. After all, the crux of the matter is Crosslyn Rise." She shot Carter a warning look. "And Crosslyn Rise is mine."

10

"YOU'RE BEING UNREASONABLE," Carter suggested, lengthening his stride to keep up with her brisk pace as they walked along the street after leaving the bank. Jessica hadn't said more than two words to him since the exchange with Gordon. "What was so terrible about my saying I want to marry you?"

"Whether we marry is between you and me. It's none of Gordon's business."

"He had a point, though. People see us together, and they wonder. Some things you can't hide. We are close. And there was nothing wrong with your deferring to me on the matter of a builder. As your husband, I'd want you to do that."

"You're my architect," she argued crossly. "You're more experienced than I am on things like choosing a builder. My deferring to you was a business move."

"Maybe in hindsight. At the time, it was pure instinct. You deferred to me because you trust me, and it's not the first time that's happened. You've done it a lot lately. Crosslyn Rise may be yours, but you're glad to have someone to share the responsibility for it." He half turned to her as they walked. "That's what I want to do, Jess. I want to help you, and it's got nothing to do with Crosslyn Rise and everything to do with loving you. Giving and sharing are things I haven't done much of in my life, but I want to do them now."

She had trouble sustaining crossness when he said things like that. "You do. You are."

"So marriage is the next step. Why are you so dead set against it?"

"I'm not dead set against it. I'm just not ready for it."

"Do you love me?"

She swung around the corner with him a half step behind. "I've been married," she said without answering his question. "Things change once the vows are made. It's as if there's no more need to put on a show."

That stopped Carter short, but only for a minute. He trotted a pace to catch up. "You actually think I've been putting on a show? That's absurd! No man—especially not one who spent years feeling second-rate, being ashamed of who he was—is going to keep after a woman the way I have after you if he doesn't love her for sure. In case you haven't realized it, I do have my pride."

She shot him a glance and said more quietly, "I know that."

"But I'll keep asking you to marry me, because it's what I want more than anything else in my life."

"It's what you *think* you want."

"It's what I *want*." Grasping her arm, he drew her to a stop. "Why won't you believe that I love you?"

She looked up at him, swallowed hard and admitted, "I do believe it. But I don't think it will last. Maybe we should just live together. That way it won't be so painful if it ends."

"It won't end. And we're practically living together now, but that's not what I want. I want you driving my car, living under my roof, using my charge cards. And my name. I want you using my name."

She eyed him warily. "That's not a very modern wish."

"I don't give a damn. It's what I want. I want to take care of you. I want to be strong for you. I resented my father because he rode through life on my mother's coattails. I refuse to do that."

Jessica was astonished. "You couldn't do that with me. I don't *have* any coattails. My life is totally unassuming. You're more dynamic than I could ever be. You're more active, more aggressive, more successful—"

He put a finger to her lips to stem the flow of words. "Not successful enough, if I can't convince you to marry me."

With a soft moan, she kissed the tip of his finger, then took it in her hand and wagged it, in an attempt at lightness. "Oh, Carter. The problem is with me. Not you. Me. I want to satisfy you, but I don't know if I can."

"You do."

"For now. But for how much longer? A few weeks? A month? A year?"

"Forever, if you'll give yourself the chance. Can't you try, Jessica?"

SHE COULD, SHE SUPPOSED, and each time she thought of marrying Carter, her heart took wing. Still, in the back of her mind, there was always an inkling of doubt. More so than either dating or living together, marriage made a public statement about a man and a woman. If that marriage fell apart, the statement was no less public and far more humiliating—especially when the male partner was Carter Malloy. Because Carter Malloy was liked and respected by most everyone he met. That fact became clear to Jessica over the next few weeks as they met with Gordon, with lawyers, with various investors. Despite Jessica's role as the owner of Crosslyn Rise, Carter emerged as the project's leader. He didn't ask for the position, in fact he sat back quietly during many of the discussions, but he had a straight head on his shoulders and seemed to be the one, more than any other, who had a pulse on the various elements involved—architectural plans, building prospects, environmental and marketing considerations, and Jessica.

Especially Jessica. She found that she was leaning on him more and more, relying on him for the cool, calm confidence that she too often lacked. Gone were the days when her life maintained a steady emotional keel. She seemed to be living with highs and lows. Some had to do with Crosslyn Rise—highs when she was confident it would become something worthy of its past, and lows when the commercial aspects of the project stood out. Some had to do with Carter—highs when she was in his arms and there was no doubt whatsoever about the strength of his love, and lows when she was apart from him, when she eyed him objectively, saw a vibrant and dynamic man and wondered what he ever saw in her.

As the weeks passed, she felt as though she were heading toward a pair of deadlines. One had to do with Crosslyn Rise, with the progress of the project, with the approach of the trucks and bulldozers and the knowledge that once they broke ground, there was no going back.

The other had to do with Carter. He would only wait so long. He'd been so good about not mentioning marriage, but she knew he was frustrated. When August came and it was apparent there would be no honeymoon, he planned a vacation anyway, spiriting her away for a week in the Florida Keys.

"See?" he teased when they returned. "We made it through a whole week in each other's company nonstop, and I still love you."

By late September, he was pointing out that they'd made it for five months and were going strong. Jessica didn't need that pointed out. Her life revolved around Carter. He was her first thought in the morning and her last thought at night, and though there were times when she scolded herself for being so close to him, so dependent on him, she couldn't do differently—particularly with the ground-breaking at Crosslyn Rise approaching fast. It was an emotional time for her, and Carter was her rock.

Even the most solid of rocks had its weak spot, though, and Jessica was Carter's. He adored her, couldn't imagine a life without her, but the fact that she wouldn't marry him, that she didn't even say that she loved him was eroding his self-confidence and hence, his patience. When he was with her, he was fine; he loved her, she loved him, he wasn't about to ruin their time together. Alone though, he brooded. He felt thwarted. He was tired of waiting. Enough was enough.

Such were the thoughts that he was trying unsuccessfully to bury when, late in the afternoon on the last Wednesday in September, he drove to Crosslyn Rise. Before Jessica had left him in Boston that morning, she had promised to cook him dinner. He hadn't spoken with her during the day, which annoyed him, since he wanted *her* to call *him* once in a while, rather than the other way around. He needed the reassurance. She wouldn't say she loved him, so he needed her to show she cared in other ways. A phone call would have been nice.

But there'd been no call. And when he opened the back door and came into the kitchen, there didn't look to be anything by way of pots and pans on the stove. Nothing smelled as though it were cooking. Jessica was nowhere in sight.

"Jessica?" he called, then did it again more loudly. "Jessica?"

He was through the kitchen and into the hall when he heard her call, "I'll be right there." He guessed she was upstairs in the bedroom—the master bedroom with its king-size bed, which she'd started using when he'd begun to sleep over regularly—and that thought did bring a small smile to his face. He was early. She always freshened up, changed clothes, combed out her hair when she knew he was coming. So she wasn't quite done. That was okay. He'd help her. He'd even help her with dinner.

Which went to show how lovesick he was. The thought of being with her, of maybe getting in a little hanky-panky before dinner was enough to wipe all the frustrating thoughts from his mind. And it wasn't just that the love-making could do it, but when they made love, he knew that she loved him. She came alive in his arms, showed him a side of her that the rest of the world never saw. No woman could respond to him—or give—in that way if she wasn't in love.

He took the stairs two at a time, but he hadn't reached the top when she came down the hall. One look at her face and he knew there would be no hanky-panky. Indeed, she looked as though she'd newly brushed her hair and changed her clothes, even put on a little makeup, but the dab of blusher didn't hide her pallor.

"What's wrong?" he asked, coming to an abrupt halt where he was, then taking the rest of the stairs more cautiously.

"We have a problem," she said in a tight voice.

"What kind of problem?"

"With Crosslyn Rise. With the construction."

He let out a relieved breath. "A problem with the project I can handle. A problem with us I can't." He reached

for her. "Come here, baby. I need a hug." Enveloping her
in his arms, he held her tightly for a minute, then relaxed
his hold and kissed her lightly. She was the one who clung
then, her face pressed to his neck, her arms trembling.
There was something almost desperate about it, which
made him a little nervous. "He-ey." He laughed softly and
held her back. "It can't be all that bad."

"It is," she said. "The town zoning commission won't
give us a permit. They say our plans don't conform with
their regulations."

Putting both hands on her shoulders, Carter ducked his
head and stared at her. "What?"

"No permit."

"But why? There's nothing unusual about what we're
doing. We're following all the standard rules, and we did
go through the town for the subdivision allowances. So
what are they picking on?"

"The number of units. The spacing of the units." She
tossed up a hand, and her voice was a little wild. "I don't
know. I couldn't follow it. When I got the call, all I could
think of was that here we are, ready to break ground, and
now the whole thing's in danger."

"No." Slipping an arm around her shoulder, he brought
her down beside him on the top step. "Not in danger. It
only means a little more work. Who did you speak with?"

Jessica looked at her hands, which were knotted in her
lap. "Elizabeth Abbott. She's the chairman of the zoning
commission."

"I know Elizabeth Abbott. She's a reasonable woman."

"She wasn't particularly reasonable with me. She informed me that the decision was made this morning at a
meeting, and that we could apply for a waiver, but she
suggested I call back the trucks. She didn't see how we
could break ground until next spring or summer at the

earliest." Jessica raised agonized eyes to Carter's. "Do you know what a delay will mean? Carter, I can't afford a delay. I barely have the money to keep Crosslyn Rise going through another winter. I'm already up to my ears in loans to the bank. The longer we're held up, the longer it will be until we see money on the other end. That may be just fine for men like Nolan and Heavey and Gould, and it may be okay for you, but for me and the rest of us—it's too late!"

"Shh, honey. It's not too late." But he was frowning. "We'll work something out."

"She was vehement."

Releasing her, Carter propped his elbows on his thighs and let his hands hang between his knees. "Small towns aren't usually this rigid with one of their leading citizens."

"I'm no leading citizen."

"Crosslyn Rise is. It's the leading parcel of land here."

"That's probably why they're being so picky. They want to know exactly who's coming in and when."

Carter shook his head. "Even the snobbiest of towns don't do things like this. Something stinks."

Jessica held her breath for a minute. She looked at Carter, but his frown gave away nothing of his deeper thoughts. Finally, unable to wait any longer, she said, "It's Elizabeth Abbott. I could tell from her voice. She's the force behind this."

He eyed her cautiously. "How well do you know her?"

"Only enough to say hello on the street. We never had anything in common. I'm not saying that she's deliberately sabotaging our progress, but she's clearly against what we're doing. She seemed pleased to be making the call, and she wasn't at all willing to even *consider* accommodating us." Jessica's composure began to slip. "They could hold a special meeting, Carter. How difficult would it be for three people to meet for an hour? When I asked, she said that wasn't done. She said that they'd be more than happy to consider our waiver at their next scheduled meeting in February." Her voice went higher. "But we can't wait that long, Carter. We can't wait that long."

Carter continued to frown, but the curve of his mouth suggested disgust.

"Talk to her," Jessica said softly. "She'll listen to you."

His eyes shot to hers. "What makes you say that?"

"Because you had something going with her once. She told me."

His expression grew grim. "Did she tell you that it happened seven years ago, when I was still living in New York, and that it lasted for one night?"

"Go to her. You could soften her up."

"One night, Jessica, and do you want to know why?" His eyes held hers relentlessly. "Because she was something I had to do, something I had to get out of my system. That's all. Nothing more. We were classmates here in town way back when. She was a witness to some of my most stupid stunts. Far more than you in some ways, she was synonymous in my mind with the establishment around here. So when she came up to me that night—it was at a reception in one of the big hotels, I don't even remember which—I had this sudden need to prove to myself that I'd really made it. So I took her to bed. And it was the most unsatisfying thing I've ever done. I didn't see her again in New York, and I haven't seen her since I moved back here."

Jessica's heart was alternately clenching tightly and pounding against her ribs. She believed every word Carter said—and the truth was echoed in his eyes—still she pushed on. "But she'd like to see you again. I could tell. Maybe if you gave her a call—"

"I'll call one of the other members of the commission."

"She's the chairman. She's the one who can make things happen, but only if she wants. Talk to her, Carter. Make her want to help us."

Carter was beginning to feel uneasy. Sitting back against the banister to put a little more space between them, he asked cautiously, "How would you suggest I do that?"

Jessica had been tossing possibilities around for the better part of the afternoon, which was why she hadn't called him earlier to tell him about the problem. The solution she'd found was as abhorrent as it was necessary, but she was feeling desperate on several counts. "Smile a little. Sweet-talk her. Maybe even take her to dinner."

"I don't want to take her to dinner."

"You take prospective clients to dinner."

"Prospective clients take *me* to dinner."

"Then make an exception this time. Take her to dinner. Wine and dine her. She'll listen to you, Carter."

"Okay. You and I will take her to dinner."

"You're missing the point!" Jessica cried.

"No," Carter said slowly. His eyes were chilly, reflecting the cold he felt inside. "I don't think I am. I think that the point—correct me if I'm wrong—is that I should do whatever needs to be done to get a waiver from the commission, and if that means screwing Elizabeth Abbott, so be it." While he didn't miss the way Jessica flinched at his choice of words, he was too wrapped up in his own emotions to care. The coldness inside him was fast turning to anger. "Am I right?"

The harsh look in his eyes held Jessica silent for a minute.

"Am I right?" he repeated more loudly.

"Yes," she whispered.

"I don't believe it," he murmured, and though his voice was lower, the look in his eyes didn't soften. "I don't believe it. How can you ask me to do something like that?"

"It may be the only way we can go ahead with this thing."

"Is that all that matters to you? This *thing*? Crosslyn Rise?"

"Of course not."

"Could've fooled me. But then, it's no wonder. You won't say you love me, you won't say you'll marry me, and now you come up with this idiotic scheme."

"It's not idiotic. It would work. Elizabeth Abbott has a reputation for things like this."

"Well, I don't. I wouldn't demean myself by doing something like this. I'm no goddamned gigolo!" Rising from the stairs, he stormed down three steps before turning to glare at her. "I love you, Jessica. If I've told you once, I've told you dozens of times, and I'm not just blowing off hot air. I love you. That means *you're* the woman I want. Not Elizabeth Abbott."

Jessica swallowed hard. "But you were with her once—"

"And it was a mistake. I knew it at the time, and I know it even more now. I won't go so far as to say that she's holding up things for Crosslyn Rise because of me, because even when she used to call me and I wouldn't see her, she was gracious. I never thought of her as being vindictive, and I'm not about to now, but I won't sleep with her." Agitated, he thrust a hand through his hair. "How can you ask me to do that?" he demanded, and through the anger came an incredible hurt. "Don't I mean anything to you?"

Jessica was so stunned by the emotions ranging over his face that it was a minute before she could whisper, "You know you do."

But he was shaking his head. "Maybe I was fooling myself. Part of love is respect, and if you respected me for who and what I am, you wouldn't be asking this of me." Again he thrust a hand into his hair; this time it stopped midway, as though he were so embroiled in his thoughts that he couldn't keep track of his gestures. "Did you honestly think I'd go along? Did you think I'd seduce her? Did you think I'd really be able to get it *up*?" He swore softly, and his hand fell to his side. "I blew it somewhere, Jessica. I blew it."

In all the time she'd known him, Jessica had never seen him look defeated, but he did now. It was there in the bow of his shoulders and the laxness of his features, either of which put him a galaxy apart from the angry and vengeful boy he'd been so long ago. She knew he'd changed, but the extent of the change only then hit her. She was still reeling from it when she caught the sheen of moisture in his eyes. Her knuckles came hard to her mouth.

"I'd do most anything for you, Jessica," he said in a gut-wrenching tone. "So help me, if you asked me to lie spread-eagle on the railroad track until the train blew its whistle, I'd probably do it, but not this." Swallowing once, he tore his eyes from hers, turned and started down the stairs.

"Carter?" she whispered against her knuckles. When he didn't stop, she took her hand away. "Carter?" Still he didn't stop, but reached the bottom of the stairs and headed for the door. She rose to her feet and called him again, more loudly this time, then started down. When he opened the door and went through, she quickened her step, repeating his name softly now and with a frantic edge. By the time she reached the door, he was halfway to his car.

"Carter?" Her eyes were filled with tears. "Carter!" She was losing him. "Carter, wait!" But he was at the driver's